LANDBOUND

DANIELLE BUTLER

For Matt

CONTENTS

Chapter 1

With "salt-washed eyes" I can "see true" and make people do what I say. At least that's what's supposed to happen.

"Try it again." Macon flicks water at my face, and I laugh.

The sun is high overhead in a blank blue sky. It's like summer. I mean, technically it *is* summer, so it should feel like it, but weather on an island in upper New England is changeable. The dry sand we're sitting on is warm enough that I don't mind when the edge of an icy wave reaches for my toes.

"C'mon, try it again!" He leans his head back and narrows his eyes like a challenge.

"Okay, okay." I hop up and splash down into the surf until the water eddies around my ankles. Yep, right into the water. Something that wouldn't have been conceivable just a few months ago. Even just sitting close, I'd be fighting a panic attack. Now I can walk right into the ocean. I have made my small peace with it.

I cup sea water in my hands and splash my face. Salt hits my eyes and the day turns even brighter. The sand glints in the sunlight; the ocean stretching away is multi-shaded, the depths darker and wave crests whiter than bone. My skin shines with a pearly cast, and I know my eyes swim with colors.

Macon smiles at me. He's so beautiful that for a moment I forget what I'm supposed to be doing. I do see Macon's true beauty—like a glow from within—but I can't make him do anything. That part of my newfound siren power hasn't worked on him yet, but we keep trying. I haven't really used it on anyone else since I got back to Maine. I don't know why he's so insistent, but at least he didn't freak out when I told him I had tried to control him before. I mean, I thought at the time that I was releasing him from any inadvertent thrall I had over him… but still. I'd have been mad if I thought someone was taking my choices away. He gives me a "get on with it" look.

"Go get me a snack," I command, feeling the salt in my eyes, the force of my will. Nothing. "Get me a towel." Macon just looks at me, grinning. I dip my hands again and wet my face. I lock eyes with him. "Kiss me."

In a second, he wraps one arm around my waist and pulls me close, his face a breath away. Then he leans in and I am caught up in his embrace, his mouth on mine.

When we break, I am out of breath. "That worked?"

"Well, no, but I didn't want to waste the opportunity."

I shake my head but can't help laughing.

"I'm going to have to go," Macon says, looking at his watch. "I'm supposed to help my mom."

"Where does she think you are?" I try to keep my tone light.

"She knows I'm with you. I just promised that I'd be home by two." I don't know what my face betrays, but he puts his hands on my shoulders as if to underline his next words. "She likes you. Or she will once she gets to know you better. It's fine."

"Yeah, I know."

He doesn't look as if he believes me, but he doesn't say anything more about it. It's as if a cloud has covered the sun.

"I want to run by the clearing really quick on my way."

The clearing isn't exactly on the way to his side of the island from here, but it feels like home to him. It's one of the most peaceful places on the island, so I can't begrudge him. I guess it's a recharge for him, the way Ellie's sea stew is for me.

"I'll see you in the morning. Meet you at your dock."

"I'll be there." A school day. Hurrah. The year has just started, and I'm still finding my way in the new school.

"Oh, I almost forgot. I made you something." He holds out his hand in a fist, hiding whatever it is.

"You did?" A pleased flush warms my face. "What is it?" I slide my hand under his, and he places a small figurine in it. It's a little, carved seahorse about two inches tall. Really intricate. He's managed to carve even the little spines decorating its back and the tight spiral curl of its tail. It has a cute snub nose and the wing-like fins are so fine, I imagine I could see through the edges. He's smoothed it well, but it still looks like new pine and carries the scent of the forest. "This is really good. It must have taken you ages."

"You like it?"

"It's beautiful. I love it."

I launch into his arms giving him an exaggerated thank you smooch. He smiles against my lips. Then he really kisses me again.

Too soon, he steps back and gives me a rueful half-smile. "Okay, gotta go. See you."

I say goodbye, and he heads east. I watch him until he

goes over the rise and then turn back to the ocean, slipping the seahorse into my pocket.

I walk a little way into the surf and splash my face again. I search the waves but see nothing and no one. Since I brought Mom back from New Mexico, I haven't seen the girl from the water again. I met her on the rocks on the south side of the island, and later she took me to the siren world—Araem, Ellie's world—for a few moments. I don't even know her name. I remember her face like a dark pearl, her silver hair, and sharp smile. I've dreamed about her a couple of times, too, but no sightings.

I haven't seen *any* faces in the waves. I was sure we heard singing the first night we got back but nothing since then. It's as if the other sirens have disappeared. Ellie says sometimes they go quiet. I don't think my grandmother would outright lie to me, but I'm sure she wasn't telling me the whole truth. What a surprise.

I've tried to get her to tell me more about Araem and those she calls sisters, but she only gives little snippets of stories. To be honest, it seems to make her sad, so I haven't pressed her. When we needed to get Mom from New Mexico, she told me that she wasn't able to leave the island—not since my grandfather, Oscar, disappeared. That makes no sense to me, but she won't say much more than that. Mom has told me what she remembers about that world, but she hasn't been there since she was a little girl. She remembers that the ground was soft and that someone taught her to paint colors in the air. I probably remember more from my short visit.

Still, the last couple of months since I got back have been pretty decent. And not just because I kind of have a boyfriend. Dang, how did *that* happen? I'm not complaining, not really, just feels... surprising. No, that's not the only thing, not even the best thing, if I'm honest. Mom has been doing good, really good. She has to use a cane and gets tired easily, but she's out of her wheelchair. And considering the state she was in back at the facility in New Mexico, even being *in* the wheelchair was a huge improvement.

Seeing her with Ellie has been an education. They held each other for five whole minutes when we got back, both crying. It was beautiful. But before long, I guess they remembered why they hadn't spoken for years. They aren't fighting now really, but let's just say that I'm glad that we are living in the house, Windemere, and that Ellie stayed in her cottage. Everything is pretty good.

I just need to make sure it stays that way. Keep positive. Make sure Mom stays healthy, that she doesn't get too stressed out. I need to focus on that. It's way more important than quiet sirens, I know. We can make our new life here work.

My phone chirps, but I don't check it. It can't be Macon texting me; he'll still be walking back. It could be Blue, but I know she's at the café this afternoon. Jane finished her research here and left a few weeks ago to go back to college in California. Besides, she was camping this weekend somewhere, as she said, "No phones can find me." Mom and Ellie were working on some hides when I left them. They won't be done quite yet. And Ellie sure doesn't send phone messages anyway.

I'm trying to time it perfectly so that they'll be finished before I get back, and I don't have to help with the hides. I just want to spend a few more minutes enjoying the walk, the heat and sun soaking into my skin, salt drying on my lips, and listening to the seagulls chattering at each other above me. I take a deep breath of sea air and along with the ocean, smell pine trees. The breath of the island.

My phone chirps again as I'm climbing back up toward

the house. My stomach churns. Persistent, that's for sure. I stop, annoyed, and finally pull out my phone. It's an email, not a text. This must be the fourth message this week.

"Cam, honey, you coming?" Mom calls me from outside our front door.

I wave and pocket my phone again without opening the email. I know I don't have to be on high alert every time he writes, and I'm not trying to ignore him, per se. It's just things are so good right now…

"What's up?" Mom asks when I get close.

"Nothing." I shrug.

"You have that look. That 'I'm gonna tackle everything myself' look."

I smile at her grumpy impression of me and try to see past it to gauge how she's feeling. She must guess what I am doing because she rolls her eyes.

"I'm fine. Stop watching me like that. Go get cleaned up and you can help me with the dinner prep."

I spot one of Ellie's baskets on the ground. "You went fishing?"

"Momma did while I was working on the skins." She purses her lips.

I don't ask why they divvied up the tasks but hurry off to the bathroom to wash my hands. Then I head across the hall into the small bedroom that I took over when we got back. I'd never really moved into the other one anyway. It's easier for Mom with her cane to be in the room connected to the bathroom.

In the privacy of my room, I pull out my phone and check the email.

Cam—this is getting ridiculous. You need to write me back. I tried calling the house, and the number is discon-

nected. I tried your cell. Your Mom's number isn't working. Where are you?

"Cam?" Mom is at my door, and I fumble the phone trying to put it away. "You all right?"

"Mom!" I groan her name and make a silly face at her, mock-rolling my eyes just as she'd done to me, phone safely in my pocket again. "I'm fine."

"Careful, your face'll freeze like that."

"Yeah, yeah. Let's go see what we're having for dinner."

I haven't told her about the emails. That Dad is finally wondering where I am. I will. Just not yet.

Chapter 2

I check my bag and pockets again, making sure I have my notebook, phone, lip balm, books, snack, and all that. I usually manage to forget something, and it's not like you can just jog home to get it. My fingers slide across a tiny bottle of sea water. I'm not planning to use it; it's just in case. I don't know "just in case" of what. It makes me feel safer, more comfortable, to have it with me. I also have the little seahorse Macon carved for me. I run my thumb over the whorl of its tail and smile.

Macon glances back at me from the driver's seat of the boat. "Come on up."

He slows the boat gently, while I make my way to him. He's been teaching me how to pilot a boat. I had to take a safety course online first, though. I settle into the seat, take the wheel, and put my hand on the throttle but don't yet increase the speed. Instead, I search the horizon while we float. I study the lapping waves looking for any flashes, any faces. I strain my ears but only hear the slosh of water. There's nothing out there. Listening to the sirens' songs, seeing their other-worldly skin and eyes, visiting Araem… It almost feels like a dream.

"Cam?"

"Yeah, I have it." I toss a smile at him. "All good."

I push the throttle forward and speed up. I take us all the way until we see Williams Point in the distance. I don't yet feel comfortable docking. Macon says I'm going to have to learn sometime, and I will. But today is not that day.

We pass Blue's café on the way to the high school, and she barrels out the door wearing an acid green coat and trying to hold three bamboo to-go cups. Macon grabs the door, and I take a dripping cup from her.

"Nice coat. Where'd I put my sunglasses? Is this for me?"

"Ha ha, and yes, so be more grateful to be served by my awesome fashionista self. One for you, too." She hands a cup to Macon.

"Goddess," I say, then take a big swig.

"That's me." She grins and flips her currently magenta hair. It kind of clashes with her loud coat, but because it's Blue she somehow pulls it off.

Macon thanks her, and they chat and joke the rest of the way to the school. I must be a little quieter than normal because at one point, Blue bumps me with her shoulder and tells me to "join the party." I laugh and make some silly comment, but my words are as empty as the sea was this morning—and has been for weeks. Macon catches my eye, but I just shake my head.

My new high school is completely different from the others I've gone to and also totally the same. I'm pretty sure the full school population is less than the last graduating class of my school in Albuquerque and you couldn't take Costal Navigation 101, but I swear it smells the same inside. It's a thing with public schools. I'm convinced they all use the same cleaning products or something.

Macon touches my elbow before he takes off to his first period class. We're not big on PDA, so no sloppy kisses in the hallway like the senior couple that always seems to be making out by the entrance to the girls' bathroom. Still that small touch sends a zing up my arm. I tell him I'll see him later and say goodbye to Blue, wishing I had first period with either of them.

Instead, I get to have it with Bridgette—Macon's overly pretty ex and the one person in our friend group who seems constantly suspicious of me. She doesn't look over as I enter the class, but I see her perfect nose wrinkle a little as she smooths her glossy, dark hair. I ignore her and go to my seat toward the back. I don't have time for whatever drama might be simmering there. With the curriculum differences from the southwest to the northeast and me missing loads of school last year due to Mom's sickness, I'm behind in a few classes. I had to test to get into this English class and still have a backlog of required reading to catch up on.

It actually isn't as bad as you might imagine—Bridgette, I mean. Since I shot her down when she labeled me a witch on the beach that day and tried to ward me off with a necklace, of all things, she hasn't said much to me. She makes comments, of course. Sharp, subtle remarks as if she's trying to get me to admit to something or get other people to realize something about me. She's been around at a few get togethers I've been to over the last couple of months. Snarky cracks and definite side-eye shade aside, she's been civil to my face, at least.

I get my notebook out and listen to Mr. Owens talk about *To Kill a Mockingbird*. I've already read it. Or rather, I listened to it. I got it from the library on audiobook last year.

Sissy Spacek was the narrator, and I was entranced with how her southern accent made the words sing. I had to look her up because I didn't know who she was. Mom was appalled that I didn't know the original *Carrie* and the million other parts she'd played.

Mr. Owens is a really good teacher. He asks interesting questions, doesn't try to be "cool" and never talks down to us. Today, though, as I lean my chin on my hand and listen, I can hardly hold onto his words. His voice is calm and almost hypnotic. He's talking about the setting being like a character, but his voice is getting lost in the sound of waves.

The ocean has turned tide, and I can hear how there's a little bit more water in each crash. Each wave bringing the sea to land, pulling back, then falling forward again, rhythmic as breathing, as blood flowing, as a heartbeat.

Suddenly, I am at the coast, on the sand, watching the ocean come in. I see a flash that could be sunlight on the waves but might be something more. I hear voices, far away but distinct, calling out. Finally! Lightness floods me, as a weight is lifted from my heart, sending effervescence through my veins. I could almost cry. I hear my name, the voice urgent, pleading with me. But I can't see anyone. I try to call back, but no sound passes my lips. The weight settles back through my body, a creeping dread. I reach out toward the surf, but there's an invisible barrier stopping me. I hear my name again, and try to push through the surface blocking my way. It's smooth and cold, like glass.

"Cam, Cam Vale!"

I jump. I'm in the classroom, hand pressed against the window, looking at a ghost of myself in the reflection. My heart is hammering inside my chest.

"Cam?" Mr. Owens is standing next to me. I can literally feel the entire class staring. Excellent. "Are you okay?"

I look up into Mr. Owens' face, embarrassed. He looks confused and strange, his brown hair has so many colors in it that I have never noticed, and his dark eyes are a richer chestnut color. That's when I realize that my cheeks are wet. I look away and blink rapidly to clear the salt from my eyes.

"You were staring out the window as if something was wrong. You didn't hear me?"

"I— I thought I saw something," I say. My face is in flames. "I'm sorry, it was just... nothing."

"Well, sit back down." He furrows his brow at me. "All right everyone, show's over. Lilly, how does Harper Lee describe the heat in Maycomb?"

Back at my desk, I wipe my face and try to concentrate on what Lilly is saying. I breathe in and out, timing my inhale to four counts and then exhale the same. I haven't had a panic attack in weeks, but I feel the buzzing in the back of my head as if one's close.

I glance up and most people are listening to Lilly, doodling in their notebooks, or trying to slyly text, but Bridgette is staring at me, eyes narrowed. She turns away pointedly when she sees me looking.

AT LUNCH, I'm distracted enough that I don't notice Luke and Diego are throwing food above me until a pretzel lands on my head.

"Ow!" It didn't really hurt but it surprised me.

"C'mon guys," Macon says to his friends, as he dusts salt from my hair.

They bust up laughing and try to apologize through giggles and crumbs.

"It's fine," I say. I smile, or think I do, but Macon gives me a funny look.

"Bathroom break," says Blue and pulls my arm.

"I don't need to go."

"I do, and you are morally and contractually obliged to come with me."

"Obliged, am I?"

"As a girl, yes." She tugs my arm again. I shrug to Macon and follow her.

When we are out of earshot of the guys, Blue pulls me into an empty classroom and demands, "What gives?"

"What are you talking about?" I shift under her laser gaze.

"You aren't acting like yourself, and I heard about this morning."

"This morn— That was a misunderstanding." A cold prickle of embarrassment creeps across my neck.

"Bridgette said you looked like you were... sleepwalking."

"She said that?"

"Well, she said, 'completely under a spell' but that's just her overactive imagination showing. So, what happened?"

I sigh. I'm at a loss. If I can't explain it to myself, how am I supposed to explain it to her? And she doesn't know anything about the sirens—about me. I haven't gotten up the nerve to explain my family history to her yet. I want to but I don't know how she'll take it, and besides, I'm still figuring it all out. Right now, I want to tell her that Bridgette made up or exaggerated this story. I want to laugh it off, but I'm a crappy liar. I search for the right words to give my impatient friend who's staring at me as if I'm going to crack under the weight of her eyes.

"I thought I saw something. I went to the window. I didn't hear Mr. Owens say my name." Three true things, I almost smile. Blue looks thoughtful, like she's going to let it go, and then I ruin it. "It was nothing."

Blue's gaze sharpens, as if she can hear my lie.

"There was nothing there." Truth.

"You're saying she was making a mountain out of a molehill?"

"Have you actually ever seen a molehill?" I laugh, kind of relieved.

"Uh, no, but whatever. So, it was nothing? That's your story?"

"Yeah…"

"Huh. Sure, okay. Whatever." She dips her head a second and then continues with calm intensity. "I know we haven't known each other forever, but you can talk to me, Cam, about anything. We're friends, right?"

"Of course."

The bell rings then, and I'm only slightly annoyed I've spent the rest of lunch getting grilled and evading Blue's questions. She throws me a half-hearted smile and waves as she leaves, but her eyes are still sharp.

Macon catches up with me in the hall. He raises his eyebrows at me.

"It's all good, I think," I say.

"Did she ask you about what happened in your English Lit class?"

Oh great. Now Macon's heard about my morning, too. "Yeah…" I reach for his hand and tug him to a stop in the flow of kids heading to class. "But I don't exactly know what happened." I lower my voice. "And there's not much I can say to Blue."

"What about to me?"

I shrug. "It was like a dream. I thought I was at the beach and someone was calling me."

"One of your travel dreams?"

That's what he calls them. Sometimes when I'm dreaming —or at least since I moved here—I find myself somewhere else. It feels real, like real things are happening, and I'm seeing them. I researched it and found out about astral projection—where your spirit travels outside your body. I guess it's something like that, but I really don't know. When I asked Mom about it, she thought I just meant very vivid dreams, so I guess she's never experienced it. Macon knows about them because one time, he saw me. One minute I was on the airplane flying back to Maine, the next I was over the water watching him. He said it was only for a second, but he saw me appear in front of him.

"Maybe like that." I hear the question in my statement. "But I think something's wrong."

"With your Mom?"

I jerk my chin toward the coast. "Out there."

Chapter 3

Time slows to a crawl for the rest of the school day. I was tempted to ask Macon to take me back to the island right after lunch, but ditching in the second week is probably a bad idea.

I get through all my classes, thankful that Ms. Dye in the art class I have with Blue gives a lecture so we can't really talk. An idea is brewing, and I don't want to muddy the waters trying to avoid Blue's questions about this morning.

After last period, I rush to the front of the school to meet Macon. I'm filled with nervous energy. Blue reaches me first. "I have an afternoon shift, want to hang out for a bit? I'll give you free syrup shots in your latte."

Macon is right behind her. He looks at me and opens his mouth, but I answer before he can say anything. "We have to get back right away today."

"Too bad, they just brought back Pumpkin Spice."

I hate Pumpkin Spice. I don't even like sugar in my coffee, much less syrup, but all I say is, "Rain check?"

Blue grouses a bit as we walk toward the coast, but then grins and waves as she heads into the café. Nothing keeps her down for long.

"C'mon," I say to Macon and quicken my pace to nearly running.

"What's the hurry?" he calls after me. As he gets closer he grumbles. "Why exactly couldn't we take Blue up on free coffee?"

"I have an idea I want to try. And it was only free syrup anyway." I make a face.

"Hey, I *like* a Salted Caramel shot. Idea for what?"

"You'll see." Then I do run the rest of the way to the dock. I don't slow until I reach the boat. I toss my bag onto the seat and climb carefully down. Macon sets about untying the boat and getting everything ready to go. Just then my phone buzzes. It's another message from Dad. I really need to write him back. I will. Soon.

At the moment, I have something else on my mind. My knees are bouncing as I wait for Macon to finish getting everything together. "Need help?"

"Nearly there. Want to tell me what's going on? You want to get back to your Mom?"

"Well, I don't want to be late for Mom."

"We're gonna be early at this rate."

He sounds a little annoyed. I can understand. We've been hanging out after school, taking advantage of time together or with our friends before we need to get back to do homework, chores, or whatever. We've gone to Blue's café a couple times, the library, and once I got in trouble for not being hungry for dinner because we went to DJ's for lobster rolls and clam chowder. Or maybe I was in trouble because I didn't bring any back.

He's finally at the wheel and starts the engine. I'm standing next to his elbow, too geared up to sit on the bench.

"I want to go to where you stopped the boat after that party… at Luke's brother's place." The party wasn't fun for me, mostly because this older guy, Theo, wouldn't leave me alone—until I *told* him to, that is. I didn't even know what I was doing—or even what I was—at the time. Bridgette was watching then too.

"There isn't exactly a sign there."

"I know but just try to get somewhere near it, okay?"

"It's too early for stargazing," he says, referring what we were doing the last time we stopped there.

Or part of what we were doing. I feel my cheeks warm, and he must guess what I am thinking because he grins and raises an eyebrow. The ride back from the party that night was much better. There, under the stars, was where we first kissed. But also, I'm also pretty sure that there's a window—a passage—into Araem in that area. One of the sirens stole my pearl earring that night and gave it to Ellie. I tug my earlobe. I still miss those earrings. Ellie gave that one back, but then I traded the pair for help. I shake my head to clear away the memories and face into the spray.

After what seems like forever, Macon slows the boat.

"This is it?"

He shrugs at me. "Near here. It's just a best guess."

"Okay, cool, stop the boat."

He cuts the engine, and I hang on to his shoulder for support while we rock in the waves, slowing down.

"Okay. What now?"

"Turn around."

"What? Why?"

"Come on, please?"

He sighs and faces away. I kick off my shoes and shimmy out of my jeans.

"What are you doing?" Macon shifts.

"Don't turn around!"

"Okay!"

I take off my T-shirt and grab the floating ring attached by a rope to the boat in one hand. "Wait here. I'll be right back," I say, and jump into the water.

I hear Macon shout just as the sea closes over my head. The force of the jump rips the lifesaver ring from my hand. The shock of the cold takes my breath away. The sea is full of colors and textures as the salt water fills my eyes. In this moment, I'm not afraid. The shadow of the boat hovers high above me. I'm sinking, but I kick my legs and rise a little. I'm searching for the shimmer of a passage window, a flash of metallic hair, anything. I don't even hear voices. Wait, that's not true. I do hear something. Like a far-off conversation, a whispered song. It's something. I turn in the water, trying to track the source of the noise.

"Hello?" I call out, or try to, around the bubbles that surround my head. It doesn't sound right. It isn't clear, just sounds as if the words are caught in air and water. I don't know how else to explain it. I could hear the girl under water before, so there must be a trick to it. I sink further, take sea water into my throat, and call again. This time my voice cuts through the ocean. I hear it in the same layered and complex way as I heard the girl, as if coming from afar but also right in my ear. "Where are you?" I call as loudly as I can.

Suddenly hands press against my mouth. "Hush." The girl is leaning from her world into ours, just as though she's leaning out of a window. Now I can see the shimmer of the passage. This one is only large enough for her head and shoulders to poke through. Her silver hair swims around her dark face, caught in the ocean's current. She looks different though, older, not much younger than me now, instead of twelve or thirteen like the last time I saw her.

"You should not shout," she says. Her voice is quiet to my hearing.

"Where have you been? I looked for you." I'm trying to make my voice soft as hers, but she winces and puts a finger to my lips.

She pulls me forward right to where the ocean water joins her world. Then she draws me even closer until I lean forward into the passage. The thick, warm air of the siren world caresses my cheek. She speaks directly into my ear. "You must be quiet. It's not safe here for you." She looks behind her. "Come see me at the water later, where we met on the rocks."

"When?" I try whispering it.

"Between the light and dark when your stars first appear."

I nod, and she turns, but I grab her hand. "Wait, what's your name?" I say as softly as I can.

She smiles. "I am Odele, sometimes Del. Go now." She disappears. The opening closes behind her.

Oh-DELL-ay. I repeat her name in my head as I kick my legs, propelling myself upward to where I can see the boat's shadow and the sun trying to pierce the ocean depth. Before I reach the surface, something crashes through next to me in a cloud of bubbles and thrashing. It's Macon wearing nothing but his boxer briefs and a rope tied around his middle. His expression morphs from fear to relief and then pure frustration when he sees me.

"Seriously, what the hell, Cam?" It's about the fifth time he's asked me. He's really pissed off. I can hardly get a word in edgewise. I'm trying to tamp down my own irritation at the third degree and trying to forget we're just wearing our underwear.

"I told you. I had an idea and just wanted to check if I

could see anything." I drop my towel and jerk my T-shirt back over my head.

"You should have told me about it first."

"I thought you'd say no."

"What am I? Your dad? To give you permission? We should have talked about it." He has his jeans back on and is rubbing his hair with his towel.

"I told you I'd be right back."

"But you weren't!"

"Jeez, Macon, it was like a minute."

He stares at me.

"What?" There's no elegant way to put on jeans over damp legs. "Can you turn around?"

"Uh, no," he says, but to his credit, he's only looking at my face. "Cam, you were gone for longer than that."

"So two minutes, then!" He's not letting me tell him the most important part. "Macon, I saw the—"

"Cam, it's been an hour. I have been out here for an hour."

"What?" I notice the sun then, that it has moved lower in the sky. It couldn't have been that long.

He pushes a hand through his hair, and I see how pale he is. "That wasn't the first time I'd gone into the water looking for you. And it's dangerous to do that on open water when you're by yourself. My dad would kill me if he knew. I dropped anchor and thank God it's shallow enough here for that to have worked. I pinned our location on my GPS too, but I wasn't sure if I did it in time, if we'd drifted." He sits heavily on the seat. "I thought about calling the Coast Guard, but how was I going to explain that I was sure you hadn't drowned?"

"I didn't know. For me it was only a moment."

"Did you go to that… to Araem?"

"No, but I saw the girl. Her name is Odele."

"She was just in the water?"

"She heard me calling to her. She, well, she kind of poked her head through. From the other side."

His brow furrows. "The time passage. We know it's different there."

"Yeah, but I didn't go in... not really." Odele had just pulled my head through, just a touch of their air. "Last time, I was there for ten minutes and you said that it was less than thirty seconds here."

"But that's not what happened this time." He huffs out a breath. "*I* don't know how it works. You should ask your Mom or Ellie. I have to get back, Cam. Tell me what happened while I drive." He looks down then and shakes his head. "Oh my God, I thought I was going to have to face Miss Ellie and tell her that I'd somehow lost you."

I try to laugh at that, but the idea is just not funny.

As we skim over the water, I tell him about my conversation and my promise to meet Odele on the rocks at dusk.

"You can't go alone."

"What do you mean?"

He pulls his eyebrows low over his eyes and shakes his head sharply, just once.

"It'll be fine. Don't be weird."

"I'm not. What if something happens? You have to at least tell Miss Ellie."

I give him a tight smile but don't answer. I don't know what Ellie would say, but I'm sure I'd be opening up a whole can of worms for no reason. I don't even know what Odele wants to tell me. And it isn't like I am going back under the water with her. Besides, Ellie hasn't seemed that worried about the silence of the other sirens.

"You know, Cam, I've been pretty cool about all of this," Macon says, slowing the boat again.

"I know."

"You can't not tell me stuff. If you're keeping secrets…"

"It wasn't a secret! I just had an idea." My hands ball into fists. I didn't mean to be gone that long. It's like he thinks I planned all this.

"It was messed up to go into the water. Five minutes ago you couldn't swim, and now you're just jumping in the ocean?"

"Look, I said I'm sorry." I grit my teeth. I don't want to fight, but he won't let up.

"It's a lot to take in. To try to figure out. It's crazy."

"Me in the water is crazy?"

"The whole thing, Cam. Everything is crazy."

I sit back on the bench then. I have nothing more to say at the moment. He's acting like… whatever. Maybe I should have talked to him first before I went in, but I had to do it. I don't know why he can't see that.

Chapter 4

I think I see Ellie on the rocks as we approach the island, but by the time we dock, she's gone. Because of our lost hour, I don't have that long until dusk. I gather my bag and am hit with regret. We've barely spoken the last half of the trip, but I don't want to leave things bad with Macon.

"Everything is going to be fine," I say. It must sound as lame as it feels to say because he doesn't look convinced. I put my bag down, step closer to him, and hook a finger in the belt loop of his jeans over his hipbone. "Come on, I said I'm sorry."

"You didn't, really. You just said that you'd said it." Still he pulls me into his arms.

"Okay, fine. I really am sorry."

"And?"

"And what?" I step back a little to look into his eyes. His hands are draped around my waist, lightly holding me in place.

"And you won't go see that girl by yourself."

Instead of answering, I lean forward and kiss him. He

doesn't kiss me back at first but then relents, pulling me closer. I don't think of anything else for a good thirty seconds.

"Camline."

I start at the sound of my name, breaking the kiss. Macon looks at me, surprised. I glance over my shoulder and see Ellie is back, standing up the path. When Macon sees her, he drops his hands and steps back with a snap.

"How long has she been there?" Macon whispers.

I shrug. He didn't hear her say my name, and quite frankly, I have no idea how I could have heard her from here. "Gotta go."

"Yeah, okay. I better run too. See you."

I grab my bag and climb onto the dock, turning back to wave at him as he speeds off. Ellie waits for me as I make my way to her. She is so still it's as if she's made of stone, a statue. Then her hair lifts in the breeze, destroying the illusion.

"Hi," I say, when I'm closer.

"What have you been doing, Camline?"

"Just coming home from school, Ellie." I avoid her gaze in case her weird siren-y power can see anything more. Maybe Macon is right, and I should just tell her about Odele and about meeting her later. There is just something about Ellie's tone that makes me hesitate. It's the sound of accusation. "How's Mom?"

"Your mother is in the cottage. She could use your help with dinner."

"Right now?" I fish my phone out of my pocket to check the time. It's still early—for dinner, anyway. It's not that long until dusk, though. I should have enough time to make it to the beach, wait for dusk, and be back in time for dinner. "Uh, I was going to go down to the water on the other side." Ellie's eyes narrow. "Just for a minute…"

"I think you have had enough water for now," she says, touching my still-wet hair.

"Oh. Well. I was just… checking something."

Ellie sighs. Her eyes soften, but she frowns at the same time. "Camline, you must be careful in the water. I have told you. You don't know the pathways. You could get lost."

"I know, I know. You did tell me." She's told me a million times to be careful—of everything from boys to water to sea urchin spines. She's just way too overprotective sometimes.

"You do not understand. This is not a good time for exploring the water. And I cannot come after you. I cannot leave… If you were to…" She stops, the pleading in her eyes changes to sorrow and then, just as quickly, hardens to ice. She turns her head away from me. "Your mother needs you now." There is finality in her words. My phone buzzes as I walk up to the cottage. I hit Ignore.

MOM IS over the stove cooking when I come in. I set down my bag and try to ignore the itchy feeling in my skin telling me to hurry, hurry down to the water. Maybe I can help her quickly and then go before we sit down to eat.

Mom smiles at me. "You're back. Great, I could use your help."

She hands me a grater and a bowl of carrots. There's a cold salad she makes with carrots and homemade lemon dressing. I love to eat it, hate to make it.

Still, I wash my hands and sit at the little table to get on with it. She checks something on the stove, covers the pot, and then comes to sit by me bringing the ingredients for the dressing, leaning her cane against the table.

As she cuts the lemons, she asks about my day and how

school is going. I don't mention waking dreams and visits with sirens. I'm concentrating on not nicking my hands on the grater when the carrots get to the ends. It's happened more times in the past than I'd like to admit. She tells me about her day with Ellie. They seem to have gotten along all right today, but Mom's mouth purses at one or two points. Maybe it's just that they were apart for too many years and have to get used to each other again. Maybe Ellie still hasn't forgiven Mom for leaving with Dad all those years ago.

I get my last carrot down as far as I can and stack it with the others when something she says snags my attention. "Hang on—you went into the water today?"

"No, I said we didn't. Momma said it wasn't a 'safe day' for it. She brought back a couple of buckets of sea water though, and I put them in the bath." I glance at her cane. She must see me do this because she adds, "It *is* helping, Cam."

"I know." I just can't forget that we nearly lost her. That I had to bring her sea water and Ellie's stew just to get her to wake up so we could take her home from the facility. She's doing so much better now. I squeeze her arm. "But what did Ellie say about a 'safe day'?" My phone buzzes, and I tap it to silence it. "What does that mean?"

"I don't know exactly. Ever since I was tiny, she would tell me to avoid the water at certain times. Something about the tides. Here, trade me." She gives me the lemons and a juice press, then takes the carrots from me.

"Huh." I balance the lemon half onto the pointed dome, press down, and turn. "The tides change every day, though." Could Ellie's warning be tied to why Odele was so nervous?

"Different tides, hon." Her hands are so steady, she can grate the carrot down to the barest sliver of the top without danger to her fingers.

I pour the lemon juice into a bowl and get up to wash my sticky hands. My phone buzzes again.

"Who is trying to get ahold of you?" Mom says and reaches for my phone.

I've gotten too used to ignoring it. "No, wait!" I turn so fast, I sling water on the floor.

"You just spent all afternoon with Macon, what could he have to tell you now?" The phone is still buzzing; Mom stares at the screen for a few seconds and then meets my eyes. "It's for you." She hands it to me. "Answer it, Camline."

I sigh and half-turn away. "Hello Dad."

Chapter 5

"Cam." He sounds relieved and maybe angry.

"Hi," I say. "How are you?"

He ignores my question. "Where are you?"

"I'm… We're in Maine."

"Your grandmother's?"

"Yeah." Mom's face is locked on mine. I can't read her expression, but I can see the muscles move in her jaw.

"When did this happen? How long have you been there?" There is static on the line, and I hear a loudspeaker in the background. An announcement or some sort of call.

"I got here in June. After Mom had to go into care." My throat closes, and no more words can get past my teeth. Cold breaks across my neck and my face goes hot. I still blame him for her getting so bad. I don't hear what he says next. "What?"

"I want to talk to your mother." There is more static on the line. I glance at Mom, her face expectant. I don't know if she heard him or is just waiting for me to hand the phone over. I don't want to—I don't know what he'll say, how she'll react. When he left us, her health went downhill. When he filed for divorce, it got worse. We can't afford another relapse. More static. "Cam? Are you still there?"

"Yeah."

Mom clears her throat and reaches out her hand. I reluctantly give her my phone.

"Go help your grandmother," she says to me. She sounds firm, but I'm afraid I detect nervousness in her tone. I hesitate. "Hello Thomas," she says into the phone. "Go on," she mouths at me, nodding her head at the door.

I leave with a huff, annoyed and worried. I can't see Ellie anywhere. She doesn't need my help; Mom just wanted me out, so obvious. I feel the pull toward the south side of the island. Soon it will be time to meet Odele. I walk six steps away from the door then stop. I'm torn between heading to the ocean and waiting to find out what my parents are talking about. I can't hear anything from inside. My toes tap a staccato.

"Camline?" Ellie calls me. Sounds like she's out near the shed.

"Coming." I drag my feet toward the sound of her voice.

She's just leaving the shed, wiping her hands on her dress. "What is it?"

"It's Dad. He's on the phone."

She nods and looks away.

"Why didn't you go into the water today?"

She slides her eyes back to mine without turning her head. "Why did you?"

I pause, irritated she won't just answer my question. My mind is still half-focused on what Mom and Dad are talking about. "I wanted to try something. We haven't heard anything, seen any of the sirens…"

"You were foolish." Her tone is scolding, and my hackles rise. "I told you…"

"You haven't told me anything!" Anger bursts behind my eyes and crackles across my skin. Ellie gives cryptic little answers, the tiniest morsels, and then expects that to be just fine. She knows so much and hardly says a thing. The frustration of months of evasion burns inside of me. I can hardly get the words past my gritted teeth. "You don't say anything. You just—"

"Stop." Ellie is still, her eyes focused on mine.

The command in her voice smacks with force and echoes inside my head. My anger pulls back, receding like water into the ocean, but then builds and returns even fuller and hits like a wave crashing. I shake off her command. "No."

Ellie takes a half step back and lets out a breath. Then she reaches forward, grasping my shoulders. I shift, but her grip is iron. She shimmers in front of me, her true self shining through. I have tears in my eyes, angry tears.

"The tides shift and the way is not always clear. You could go the wrong way, especially now when it is not safe. You must not rush head-first into what you do not understand." She looks down and then up again. "You are very strong, Cam. It will intrigue them; they might want it for themselves."

"What does that mean? You never tell the whole story!"

She slides her hands down my arms and takes my hands. "I tell what you need to know." She drops my hands, touches my cheek.

I step back. "You don't."

She just gives me one of her inscrutable looks and walks back toward the shed. I shouldn't expect any more than this, right? I mean, why on earth would my alien grandmother give me any answers? I stomp back to the house and can hear Mom talking through the door. I can't make out any words, but her voice sounds fairly calm so that's good. Fine, I'm going to head down to the south side. Just as I turn, Mom's voice gets louder and the door opens. She holds out the phone. "He wants to say goodbye."

I take my cell, and a burst of static crackles through the line. "Dad? You still there?"

"Yes, can you hear me?" His voice is broken, as if he's losing signal.

"Yeah, I'm here, Dad."

"Take care, kid. I'll call when I'm—"

The line goes dead. I glance back at Mom. "I lost him."

"Yes, well, you can talk to him again soon." There's the tiniest quaver in her voice. "He's coming here."

WE FINISH the cooking while Mom tells me about Dad's plans to visit. She isn't exact on the timing and not even sure where he was calling from. He has taken tour after tour overseas, and sometimes the military won't let him say exactly where he is. It's been years since we've seen him in person. I keep trying to gauge Mom's response, see how she's feeling about it, about him. I ask her so many questions, she finally snaps that "we will know soon enough." Then we take all the food up to Windemere to eat at the bigger table.

When Ellie joins us, Mom tells her about the call. Ellie listens, her hand hovering over her fork until Mom finishes. "He's coming here?"

"He wants to be sure we're okay—that Cam is okay." Mom flushes, like saying the last bit is admitting something. I can't let Dad get under her skin again. She nearly died. I know it couldn't have been all Dad's fault, but he didn't help.

Ellie finally picks up her fork and spears a piece of fish so hard the tines clink against the ceramic plate. Mom cuts everything into small pieces and then into even smaller ones. I'm already halfway done with my food. I'm not hungry; it tastes of nothing. I don't want to hear any more about Dad. I watch the window as the light fades. Ellie's teeth click together as she chews.

I scrape the last bit of salad into my mouth. "That was great, Mom. I'm gonna take a walk, okay?" I'm already out of my seat, taking my dishes to the sink.

Mom snaps to attention. "Camline Vale. Sit down."

She startles me, but I return to my chair, suppressing an eye roll.

"We are still eating."

When we ate as a family with Dad, we had rules about "appropriate table behavior"—no elbows on the table, no chewing with your mouth open, and no leaving the table until everyone is finished. Things have been more lax lately, but I guess the mention of Dad is enough to bring it all back in force.

By the time Mom finally lays her fork and knife down, the sun has already set. There is still a little light in the sky. I'm shifting my weight from side to side and barely stopping myself from tapping my fingertips on the table.

Mom sighs. "Good heavens, Cam, go take your walk."

I shoot out of my chair and grab my coat. "Just leave the dishes, Mom, I'll clean up when I get back."

She shoos me with a hand and shakes her head.

Ellie's sharp eyes narrow at me. She looks like she's considering forbidding me to go, but she just says, "Don't go in the water. Remember what I said. Be careful."

"Always!" I grin and then rush out the door before anyone can say anything else.

Chapter 6

I get to the south coast as fast as possible and climb down the rocks. It's dark enough that I need my phone's flashlight, holding it between my teeth to keep my hands free. Just as I drop off to the flat area, I hear my name.

Macon is at the top of the rise above me. I look from him out to the ocean. I hear the waves break against the rocks farther away. The sea is black. My flashlight doesn't even reach all the way out to the far rocks.

"Cam! Come on. What are you doing?" He calls out to me as he climbs down.

My jaw clenches. The only reason he's here is because he doesn't trust me to make my own decisions. I shine the light back toward the ocean and think I see a flash. I step toward it just as Macon reaches me and takes my hand.

I don't have time for this. The sea calls to me; I have to know what's going on and I am going to miss Odele. "What are you doing here?"

"You promised me. Guess I was right not to believe you."

I whip my hand back. "I didn't promise you anything, and

you are not my dad, Macon," I say, throwing his own words back at him.

"Come on, don't…"

"Don't tell me what to do! This is important. Why can't you understand that?"

He huffs and shakes his head. The disappointment and worry in his eyes hit me, but I can't sit here reassuring him right now. The sky is dark enough that I can already make out constellations. I may already be too late.

"Look, I'll be back in a sec. I just want to talk to her." I turn away and shine the light back toward the sea. I definitely see a flash further out and scramble toward it. My phone light bounces along, revealing rocks and small tide pools. I hurry but am trying to be careful so I don't fall flat on my face. The surf gets louder, and as one really big wave breaks, I feel the splash from where I am. I hesitate, looking for the best way to get to the ocean itself.

Macon catches up with me then. "I'm coming with."

I barely glance at him. He's going to do what he wants anyway. And I'm too focused on my little mission. I push on over the rocks. Another big wave breaks and water eddies around my feet, soaking into my sneakers. Just a little further. I see another flash in the water. She's here.

"Hello?" I call out. "Is anyone there? Odele—Del? Are you there?" There is movement in the water. I set my phone on a higher rock and then bend down to splash my face. Everything sharpens and the colors heighten. It's as if the sky lightens, but the stars don't dim, sparking through the evening sky like diamonds. I move even closer to the surf. I can see with absolute clarity each rock and the tiny sea life sloshing in the pools. Two waves break in succession, and I glimpse Odele's silver hair. I reach for her.

"Cam—be careful!" Macon shouts over the noise of the water.

Another face appears farther back and to the side of Odele, one I have never seen before. She is older and more alien. But she looks… familiar somehow. Odele glances over her shoulder, and I see fear cross her face as she disappears under the water. Another wave breaks and the new siren is closer, reaching for my outstretched hand, her gaze intent on my face.

"Come here," she says to me. The command lands like a fishhook through my breastbone, and I jerk forward as if caught. I take one halting step. The need to do as she says is almost overwhelming. I hesitate. Her mouth parts and her face hardens. Then Macon flings his hand in front of me, as if to protect me. She darts her eyes toward him for a split-second. Then the siren locks eyes with me, and her hand clamps down on Macon's wrist. With one smooth movement, she pulls him off his feet and into the water.

Chapter 7

I don't think but dive straight after them, scraping my knee through my jeans in the process. I have to push myself away from the rocks because the incoming waves try to slam me back. In the churning water, I see bubbles stream and follow them until I catch up with the siren. Macon is thrashing, his legs kicking and free hand trying to pull hers off of him. He's going to drown.

I pull water into my throat and yell, "Stop!" It makes the layered sound but no difference. Then she and the top half of Macon disappear into nothing. There's a large, roughly square cutout in the ocean. I see the telltale shimmer of a passageway. She's dragging him through a window. I follow after them as fast as I can. It doesn't matter that I never actually learned to swim. Underwater, I am graceful; I move through the ocean like a knife. I grab Macon's kicking foot and tumble with him into the siren world, into Araem.

Once we're through, the siren releases Macon's wrist. He's on the ground coughing. I'm smacked in the face with the thick air of this world. I breathe in, acclimating my lungs.

Macon's having a harder time catching his breath. I crouch by him, putting myself between him and the siren. My muscles already bunching, ready if I need to stand, to fight. My heart kicks and a cold sweat breaks out across my neck.

I glance at Macon. He wipes his hand across his wide eyes and bares his teeth in a grimace. I can see fear eating at the edges of his expression. His coughing slows a little. I have one hand on his shoulder but am mainly focusing on the strange siren.

She stares at me. "Look at you, then." Her words are spaced, deliberate, and her accent is similar to Odele's, like she's not used to the words.

Her golden hair has silver streaks—actual metallic silver, not grey or white. She has bits of jewelry woven into it, pulling it off of her face. The rest of her hair moves around her, as if it's caught in a breeze. Dense air lifts it, just as I'm sure it's doing to mine. The unknown light glints off her jewelry, making it sparkle. Her skin is pearlescent, forehead high over her multi-colored swimming eyes. She wears a dress that shimmers with the rainbow of an oil slick, and her feet are bare. Shining tattoos snake up her ankles and circle her wrists. As she quirks her mouth in a small smile, it hits me. She reminds me of Ellie.

"Who are you?" I ask.

"What's going on?" says Macon at the same time. He stumbles as he stands but straightens. "Are you okay?" he asks me.

The siren swivels her head to focus on him. I try to move in front of him, but it's like he has the same idea and tries to get in front of me. We just end up bashing against each other. I grab his hand and risk another glance at him. In the strange light of this place, he looks lit from within, just like when I have salt in my eyes, only here it's more intense. Green and brown war in his hazel eyes. His black hair floats a little away from his face, as if he's underwater. I mean actually still in the water. He meets my eyes for a fraction and then looks back to the siren. Her laser focus is on Macon, her eyes alight with calculation, with interest—far too much interest.

"And what might you be?" she says, her voice low but clear. "You don't belong here. You barely belong there."

"Hey," I say, trying to get her to stop staring at him. I'm also trying to mentally gauge exactly where we came through. I don't dare take my eyes off of her.

She flicks her glance back to me. "You are one of ours?" Before I can flinch, she grabs my arm and runs a thumb over the pearly sheen on my skin. Then she drops my wrist. "Almost." She says it with a sneer. She calls out something, somewhere between a bark and a word.

Two wiry males seem to materialize out of thin air. Goosebumps travel the length of my spine. I haven't been paying attention. We're not alone with her. Along with the two males, there is a small crowd of people—sirens—watching us. I've never seen so many in one place. I've never seen males before, ever. Each siren is different, a few are willowy and tall, others smaller with rounded limbs, some muscled like athletes. They are all other-worldly with metallic glints in their hair and pearly skin in all hues—dark to light, red, gold, and the greenish tinge of the males next to us. Their clothes—tunics, dresses, short pants—range from deep purple-black and burnt orange to softer pastels of pale blue and sherbet yellow, one shift is nearly translucent. Whatever the color, each bit of cloth seems to refract the weird light. Some sirens wear shells linked together as bracelets or neck-laces. Many have jewelry woven into their hair or pinned to their clothes. The crowd watches us as if they think we may do something entertaining, or frightening. I glimpse silver hair in the crowd, but it's not Odele. They shuffle nearer, cutting off where we came through the passage. The window hangs in the air, half obscured by an emerald-haired male and bronze-haired female. We might have been quick enough to get away from one siren to go back through, but with this many…

My attention is pulled back to the two males right next to us. They each have copper hair and the same dark, pooling eyes and skin tinged with green. They must be brothers. Their close-fitting tunics, hanging over leggings, have an iridescent sheen that reminds me of insect wings. It looks like they are wearing uniforms. Long weapon-like twin staffs are strapped across their backs, the ends jutting up above their shoulders. Guards? Something like that. We seem to warrant one apiece. They stand close but don't put their hands on us.

"Take them to the cave," the siren tells them. Then she turns to us and commands, "You will go. You will not be trouble. You will wait for me to attend you." I feel the power in her voice. Macon shifts next to me, but I don't dare look at him. I squeeze his hand.

My heart sinks. I wonder how long we've been gone back on Earth, but I just say, "Okay," as if her words have affected me. Macon starts a little, but I grip his hand again, willing him to play along. I catch him nodding in my peripheral vision.

The guards flank us, one slightly ahead and the other just behind. The one in front gestures to where rocks rise up in an outcrop. We follow, hand in hand as if we have no choice but to do as she's told us. In the back of my mind, a storm of emotions swirl. We need to get out of here. There's no way to tell how long we'll be gone. We should run, but my feet just march forward.

To be honest, I am fighting her words with everything I have. They lay on me like wet wool pushing my thoughts to agree, to obey. Part of me wants to go, to be no trouble, to wait for her. I feel sick.

Chapter 8

We make our way across the spongy ground. Even though my mind is frantic with the fact that I have no idea where we're going, it's hard not to stop and stare at everything. This is the first time I have seen so much of Araem. It's the first time I've really been here since I knew what it was called. My eyes dart around looking for the source of light in the muted sky. I don't see a sun or anything obvious, but it is light outside. Everything has that gauzy look, though. It's like everything is a watercolor painting.

The ground is full of overlapping colors made up of the reddish-brown ground and little plants or shrubs. My shoe hits against a patch of purple and it releases a puff of violet. Little motes swirl around my foot, trail after me for a second, and then dissipate. We pass a copse of— I don't know what to call them. They are almost like delicate filigree trees with connected branches and twisting roots. A small creature hides at the base of one. I just make out a flit of color from the corner of my eye, a suggestion of movement, and then it's gone. The trees wave as if in slow motion in the dense air. I want to touch them, to feel if they are as soft as they look. My hand twitches, but I don't know if that would be classed as "being trouble."

It's so quiet. Last time I was here I heard singing, but right now there is no song, no laughter. There is a slight undercurrent of sound, like white noise, wind through leaves or water far away. Our footfalls are swallowed up by the ground, and the guards say nothing to us.

Then I notice I do hear one thing: Macon breathing. It's labored, as if he's been walking uphill or running. I glance at him. His cheeks are flushed, but he still has that underlying glow. His expression is rigid. His dark hair floats around his head, and the green in his irises gleams. My eyes linger on him until he catches me looking. He half scowls, flicking his eyes forward.

We've arrived at the cave, as the older siren called it. Rocks rise up before us as tall as a house. There is an opening or doorway of sorts leading into the interior. The guards gesture inside, one walks ahead as Macon and I follow through. The doorway leads to a short tunnel that opens up into a big round room. It's a living area of some kind. There are several small windows circling the upper area so light filters through. There's a couch or bench that seems to be sculpted out of rock, the seat covered in soft-looking cushions and cloths. Near it is a raised flat table, again made from rock. On it is an opaque pitcher and some cups. One of the guards pours out a clear liquid into two cups and motions us toward them. He then takes something from a recessed shelf. It looks like a gemstone the size of a potato. He blows on it and it glows, brightening the whole area. He sets it on the table, motions again to the glasses, and then walks out.

Macon's breath is fast and urgent. He drops to the couch and leans his elbows on his knees.

"Are you okay?" I ask.

"The air. It's too. Heavy."

He looks dizzy. I take in a deep pull of the strange air and remember my first time here. The air is thick, as if it has substance—not just, well, air. I'm fine, but Macon's face is pale under the redness of his exertion.

"Let's try something," I say and start to press my mouth to his.

He pushes me back with a half-laugh. "Not now."

"Good grief, Macon, I'm not trying to make out with you. Just trust me." I breathe in again and press my lips to his, pushing my breath into his mouth. He takes it in. I sit back as he breathes out. Then I repeat it, like I am doing mouth-to-mouth in reverse, giving him the wet air I have processed into his lungs.

His breathing calms. "That's a little better. Thanks." He looks around. "Where did they go?"

"I'm not sure. Hang on." I leave him there while I creep back down the tunnel, slowing down even more when I reach the opening. Heart hammering, as if I'm doing something wrong, I peek around the edge a bit, ready to pull back at the first sight of the guards. No one stands at the mouth of the cave. I ease the rest of the way out of the doorway. All is quiet, no one is there. But I see something that we may be able to use.

"Where'd they go?"

I jump because I hadn't heard Macon walk up. I whisper back, "I don't know. They just disappeared."

"Makes sense."

"What do you mean?"

"If they thought we were compelled to do as that scary lady told us, why need guards at all? Is that why you wanted to pretend?"

"Yeah." But I still feel her words sticking to me. "I didn't want to give away that it didn't work on you. I didn't like the way she was looking at you. Didn't want to give her any more reasons to be interested in you." I shiver.

Macon coughs. I give him another lungful of breath. "How's that?"

"Better."

I nod, but I'm not sure how long it will last. "Do you see that shimmer hanging in the air?" I point to the middle distance away, past the cave's end and near another copse of tree-like things.

"Yeah. What is it?"

"I think it's a window—a passage—a way back to our world."

"Let's go," he starts to edge past me.

"Wait," I hiss and pull him back.

"What? We should go before *she* shows up." A shudder runs through his body. His breathing quickens again and he coughs.

"I know." But I'm supposed to wait here, not be any trouble. I clench my jaw.

"Are *you* all right?"

I shake my head but say, "I'm fine." I give him another breath. "Look, I don't know where that window leads. Not exactly. I don't understand how our worlds are connected. I know the ocean is the portal, but what if we end up in the middle of the Atlantic?"

I watch his face fall as he takes in my words.

We argue for a moment in low voices, moving back inside the interior of the cave. Macon suggests I go and check where the window goes, but I can't risk it. What if I can't find my way back? Or what if it takes too long? He literally cannot breathe without me. I think it's best to stick together and try to make our way back to where we came in.

"How? Do you remember where that was? And there was a ton of... people."

I don't say anything. He's right. He looks angry but underneath that, I can see the raw edges of panic. I hate seeing the look on his face. It makes me madder at myself. Because this is totally my fault. He wouldn't be here now struggling to *just breathe* if not for me. I had to run off—caught up in trying to find out what was happening with the sirens. And I have the niggling thought that she took him because I hesitated on the rocks. Whatever the reason, here we are.

Macon sits back down on the couch. He picks up a cup and sniffs the contents then sets it back on the table. He waves me over. I sit down next to him and give him another breath. I think it's getting worse.

Indecision pulls at me. I don't know exactly where we came through. There aren't enough places to hide on the way back to where we were, anyway. As soon as we leave the cave, we'll be exposed.

And we're supposed to wait.

No. I can't think like that—as if I have to do what she told me. The window outside is so close, but I can't be sure where it will lead. It could make everything worse. But just sitting here isn't doing anything. We could head back the way we came, maybe... My thoughts chase themselves like manic puppies after their tails. The image makes me laugh.

"Cam?"

Macon looks at me like I'm crazy. Maybe I am, because this is nuts. "Sorry. I don't know, Macon. I'm really sorry. I just wanted to talk to Odele."

"This is who I need to thank for your visit?"

The siren has arrived.

Chapter 9

I stand immediately. Macon gets up a fraction slower. I grab his hand. The siren holds herself straight as an arrow, again I am reminded of Ellie. She crosses to us, stopping about six feet away. Macon interlaces his fingers with mine and we hang on tight, not sure what will happen next.

"Be still," she says, her face impassive as if expecting to be obeyed.

The command is gentle but insistent, reaching out to cover me like silk instead of wool. We don't even shift. The siren's eyes land on the table, the cups, and turn to me. As her gaze crawls over my face, a small crease forms between her brows and her eyes narrow. Macon coughs then, capturing her attention. She cocks her head and watches him. I hardly dare move, even breathe. But he is struggling. He trembles and then gasps—like he can't quite get enough air.

Because that's exactly what's happening.

His grip tightens and he gasps again. I can't pretend anymore; I can't stay still any longer. I take a deep breath and turn to Macon, pressing my mouth against his. The air rushes out of my lungs into his and he relaxes. I do it again for good measure before I turn back to the siren. She has moved closer to me, and I step back in surprise. My calves hit the stone bench. There's nowhere to go.

"It is not easy for him. He is not like other... humans. He cannot survive here," she says, as if she has made a very interesting discovery. "But you can give him breath. I wonder how long that could last." She crosses her arms as if she's settling in to wait. Macon coughs again.

"Please. Let me take him back."

She doesn't waver, her focus pinpointed on Macon. He coughs and then breathes in two quick breaths. It *is* getting worse. Cold floods my chest.

"See? He needs to be out—away from here. We can't stay. Please."

"Stop talking."

The command is forceful, and my teeth snap together. The click resonates in my skull until it trips the trigger wire of my anger. I am furious at her casual interest in his suffering, in her arrogance that everyone should obey her commands. I'm angry at myself for causing all of this. My rage crackles, unwinds, and then bursts out in a single word.

"Enough." I spit the word at her, breaking any strands of her command. I take a deep breath and give it to Macon. Back to her, "Let us go."

She pulls away from me, rearing back, her mouth dropping slightly and eyes wide. I get the feeling that she's not used to being surprised. I don't care.

She closes the gap between us in an instant, grasping my chin in a vise grip and tilting my face toward hers. My anger turns back to fear as we lock eyes, and the world drops away. The sound of raging water fills my ears. I am spinning, caught in her swimming eyes, colors moving. My heartbeat echoes inside my head. I'm falling, rushing toward the ground, and then jerk as if waking in a dream just before impact. It breaks our connection; she releases my face and steps back. But as she pulls herself up, I have the distinct impression that she is shaken.

"You—you cannot leave…" It's not a command but a whisper.

"I have to." My voice is as quiet as hers, but my words are iron. I am coming back into myself, shaking off the last vestiges of her pull. Macon gasps again. I give him a breath, then another. To the siren, I say simply, "Please."

She studies me, then Macon. "He can go. You stay."

"No," Macon says.

The siren smiles, showing her sharp teeth, and commands, "You will go." Her power is immense.

Macon stands his ground, even as he struggles with air. "I won't. Leave. Without her." His jaw tightens. There is no pretending now for either of us. I may struggle against her commands, but her words mean nothing to him.

She seems to realize it, taken aback that her command didn't stick. Her face goes cold. "You…" She doesn't finish her sentence.

"I need to take him," I say, tearing her focus back to me. "He could die." My voice breaks at this, and it just makes me angry all over again. I hate having to beg her. Macon coughs again and sucks at the air like he's having an asthma attack.

She looks back to me, searching my face, and almost seems… hurt. She sags slightly and something shifts in her, I see it happen. It is as if some internal string loosens and then tightens, pulling her spine back upright.

"You cannot get back now. You would not be safe." She raises a hand as I open my mouth to protest. "But, I can help him. Better than you."

"How? Okay. Do it."

"I *could* do it."

Of course. That's exactly how I lost my pearl earrings when I needed something from Odele. Stupid sirens with their bargains. I touch my earlobes, but I'm not wearing earrings today, not wearing any jewelry. "I don't have…" I start before she interrupts.

"I don't want anything from you except a promise."

"What kind of promise?"

"Cam. Don't. Trust." Macon's words are heavy with effort, his face reddening with exertion.

I give him a breath, and as I move back, he shakes his head slightly. I am not as effective as I have been. He is struggling more. I have to get him out of here, and quick. Unless the siren can do something to help. Some siren-y, magic-y something. This is ridiculous, but I can't watch Macon suffocate. "Okay."

In a second, she is between us; she takes my arm and flicks it over.

"You will come when I call." With the tip of her finger she traces something on the inside of my wrist. It burns.

Then, moving me out of the way, she grabs Macon by the back of the neck. He shouts, and I pull at her to get her away from him. She is so strong; even with all my weight, I make no difference. With her free hand, she makes a hollow shape with her fist, pressing one side to Macon's mouth and hers to the other. Like blowing a trumpet, she pushes her siren's breath inside him. His chest inflates with the force of it. Then he drops to the couch, like a marionette with cut strings.

"Cam…" he says before he slumps onto the bench.

I rush to his side as the siren calls out to her guards. I'm certain she's killed him, but then I see his blinking eyes and chest rising and falling with rhythmic precision. "What did you do?"

"I helped."

The siren's face is closed as if carved from stone and just as impassive. She looks down at us with apparent cool detachment, but something else is there too. I can't quite place it. I am about to say something when the two guards come back in.

"Good. Keep them here." They nod but exchange glances with each other. It seems to annoy her. "Stay by the door." They appear a little confused but head back down toward the front.

"Wait a minute. You have to let us go."

"You cannot leave now. I have told you."

"We have to get back." Panic starts to creep into my voice. "You aren't listening!"

If the guards annoyed her, then I send her over the edge. Her composure crumbles and her teeth flash as she says, "You do not listen. I have told you. You cannot rush headlong into what you do not understand."

My mouth drops open. I have heard these same words before—many times—and just earlier today. The shape of her brow, the way she tilts her head, the little quirk of a smile— It's so clear. "Just like Ellie." I say it under my breath.

The siren snaps her head to me and narrows her eyes as a tremble moves through her. "We do not speak of my daughter."

Chapter 10

I'm dumbstruck as I watch her walk out. My great-grandmother. It doesn't seem possible. But then again, I am in a cave in an alternate world filled with freaking sirens somewhere in the ocean. Macon mumbles something. I brush his hair off his forehead. Then his eyes fly fully open and he sits up, nearly knocking me back in the process.

"Are you okay?" he asks me.

Hysterical laughter presses against my throat. "Are you?"

"What happened?" He is fully awake now and on high alert.

"She did something. To help you. How do you feel?"

He takes a deep breath. "I'm fine. But we're still here."

"The guards are outside."

"What did she do to *you*?"

He touches my wrist with his fingertips and suddenly, I am reminded of the burning sensation again. Where she touched me is a mark, a spiral. Precisely drawn, it looks like it was made with phosphorescence, glinting in the glow of the gem-light from the table. The skin around it is pink, healing. I rub my other hand across it. It doesn't fade, but it stings less.

"Yeah. I think it's a reminder." He frowns, and I continue, "It had to be done, Macon."

He doesn't say anything immediately, but his jaw clenches like he wants to say a lot of things. He takes another easy breath, and I wonder if he's quiet because he knows that there was no other choice for me but to make the bargain. He sighs. "So, we're prisoners?"

"Uh, well, I guess so." The siren had tried to make Macon leave earlier, but now she seems to want to keep us both here. She said it wasn't safe. I wonder if it has to do with the lack of effect that she had on Macon. Or that she could tell I was able to fight her. Or maybe she recognizes Ellie in my face, too.

Macon gets up and paces around the room. He crosses the room and then crosses back again. "How long have we been gone, Cam?"

"I don't know. We've been here an hour, maybe?"

"Which could mean anything." He drums his fingers across the walls as he starts to pace again. He starts picking things up that have been left on the sparse shelves. "We have no idea." He picks up a gem and blows on it. It flickers but doesn't glow like the other one. He squeezes it in his fist. "Didn't Ellie tell you anything about the way time moves? Or your mom?"

"No." Irritation simmers. I should have asked more questions. Demanded more answers.

He sets the gem back and runs a hand over the wall. "It's smooth. As if it was sanded down. I have never seen rock like this." He comes back to me and lifts a cushion, rubbing the edge between his thumb and forefinger. "Everything is damp but dry at the same time. I don't get it. What's this made of? What's inside? Where are we?"

I have no answers for him. I watch his face, afraid his

breathing will change again. A weight settles inside my bones dragging me back into my seat. It's too much to take in. I didn't mean for us to end up here. I just wanted to talk to Odele…

Then as if I have conjured her, I hear her voice. "You! Cam, come here!" It's whispered with force, but I can't see where it's coming from.

"There," Macon points to the ceiling.

Above us, at one of the round openings, Odele peeks through. The window is too small for her to come in but she waves me closer.

"What are you doing?"

She shushes me, darting her eyes toward the hallway.

I pitch my voice lower. "Where were you?"

Macon overlaps me, just as quiet. "Can you get us out of here?"

It is the better question.

"It is not safe."

"Everyone keeps saying that," I grumble, mostly to myself.

"Wait—you must pretend you do not know me," she hisses, but before I can ask what she means, she disappears from sight.

"Well, that was helpful," Macon says, as he continues to pace.

I go to the opening of the tunnel leading outside and listen. I can't hear the guards. Maybe they've left again. I creep down the path, conscious of every sound I make. As I near the entrance, I see the shadows of the guards and then am surprised by Odele's voice. She's out of sight, and I can't quite make out what she's saying. There is a muffled exchange and something seems to be decided because the voices get louder. They are heading toward me. I scuttle back down the hall and motion to Macon. We meet back by the table and watch as Odele comes through followed by a guard. She is carrying a tray with covered dishes that she sets on the table.

"No one should be in here, except the strangers," says the guard in a voice like gravel.

"I am supposed to leave this here for the strangers," she says in an imperious tone. "But I do not think you should be here, Kerin, is that correct? Are you not meant to be outside with Kiyash?"

The guard, Kerin, glances at us and seems confused. He appears uncertain, as though he's warring with himself about what the older siren told him to do and the sudden appearance of Odele, full of instructions. She turns her back to him, gives me a warning look, and starts to fuss with the plates as if dismissing him. He stares at her back for a moment and then grimaces in my direction but leaves. Odele peeks over her shoulder and once he disappears down the tunnel, she lets out a sigh and sits down.

"What have you done?" she asks me.

"Me? Nothing! We just went where she told us, but we really need to get back."

"The tide has not yet turned." She says it like it should be obvious, and I should know what she is talking about. "Why did Lyrionna let that one stay?" She juts her chin toward Macon.

"That's the scary lady's name?" he asks.

Odele laughs. Here the tinkling glass sound of her laughter is different, still musical but less sharp. It fades as she cocks an ear toward the tunnel. I don't hear anything.

When Odele answers him, her voice is quieter. "Yes, that is her name. She is important. She never does anything without a reason. I heard from outside—I heard her tell you to go. You spoke and then she changed her mind." She says the last as if it's completely incomprehensible.

"I don't have to—" he starts, but I cut him off.

"That's not important." I am still reluctant to advertise Macon's resistance to siren commands. "She can't keep us here. We have to get back."

Odele does an exaggerated shrug, like she's mimicking something she's seen but doesn't quite understand what it conveys. I'm struck again by the change in her in the last few months from when I first saw her. She definitely looks like she's almost my age now.

"What were you going to tell me?" I ask. "Where have you been?"

"I was afraid Lyrionna saw me at the coast. I wasn't supposed to be there at this time, so I hid."

"Right, but before—the last few months. I haven't heard singing and haven't seen you, or any of the others."

"Is this the most important thing right now?" Macon asks in a harsh whisper. "What if Lyri-whatever's 'help' wears off? I need to get back. We need to go."

I nod, he's right, but Odele does another exaggerated shrug and rolls her eyes.

"You *land boy*," she says as though handing out the harshest insult she can think of. "You could get killed—or her!—if you go at the wrong time." She looks pointedly back at me and answers my previous question. "We were only quiet because the tide had turned. We do not sing, and we should not be traveling during this."

"The tide turned? For months?" It doesn't make sense.

"Sometimes it takes that long. It has been years this time." She looks for a moment like the little girl I first met, and continues. "Then you go into the water shouting for anything to hear. I came to warn you when I thought it was safe."

"How did you know it was safe?" Macon asks, the emphasis clear on the last word.

Odele shifts under our combined focus. "I trusted chance." Her voice is small, and she lifts her chin as if preparing for us to reprimand her.

I realize then that she must have sneaked out. Whatever the "tide turning" actually means, it definitely meant that she was supposed to stay put and not be skulking around the ocean.

A loud *boom* reverberates from outside, and the ground beneath us begins to shake. I'm thrown off balance and crash into the table.

Odele's face turns to terror. "It is not possible! They are coming!"

Chapter 11

Another *boom* hits and we're all knocked off our feet. A crack runs down a wall and the gem-light falls off the table.

"Come on!" I shout to the other two as a piece of stone falls from the ceiling.

Macon is already on his feet. Odele rises as well, her frantic eyes shooting around the room. I pull her along with us as we make our way through the tunnel. Outside, Kerin and the other guard, Kiyash, are focused on trying to calm a group of sirens who have come up to them, shouting questions. People run in the background. No one seems to know where they are going or what to do. There is a quiver in the air, like ripples in the surface of a lake.

"This is our chance," Macon says to me.

In the midst of the melee, we run. I hear Odele call my name, but I ignore her. I pray we're going the right way. I only have a vague idea of where the window we came through is. Sirens are everywhere, but they are so frantic that they ignore us. One bumps me and I am flung to the ground. Macon pauses, but I get up in an instant. A flock of—something—flies right at our heads, and we duck out of the way, barely pausing. I get an impression of wings and scales, but there's no time to wonder. We pass the tree copse I remember from walking to the cave. I slow down then, tugging at Macon's hand. He is puffing.

"It can't be far from here. We have to keep an eye out." He nods, his cheeks flushed. "Are you okay?"

"Fine—keep looking."

I don't like the strain I hear in his voice. I can't see the shimmer of the window anywhere. Have we gone too far? A group of guards runs across our path farther up. I shift direction before they pay much attention to us and nearly smack us into several sirens running the other way. Just then another *boom* hits, shaking the ground, and we all tumble together. Macon and I are split for a moment. As we struggle to our feet, one of the sirens points at us. Her emerald hair swims around a face twisted with fear.

"Strangers!" she screeches.

It's as if they all suddenly notice us then. They talk over each other saying, "It's their fault! Land people."

One male with gold hair holds up a hand to us and says, "Stay away."

There is power in his voice but it washes over me like nothing and doesn't even touch Macon. Just beyond him, I see a shimmer that could be another window. It's higher in the air than the one we came through, and it's a rectangle shape instead of square. I step forward to get a better look, and the male's eyes widen. He must realize that he didn't affect us. Two others with him seem to have the same idea because in a snap, they are on guard. They fan out around us, crouching slightly as if they are ready to fight.

"We don't mean any harm," I say.

"Your kind always brings trouble, but you never 'mean' to," says a female, baring her teeth.

"Just let us go." Macon pushes in front of me.

I turn until we're back to back because two more have circled around behind us. They are muttering about everything being our fault and that they should throw us out. In the distance, I see the some of the guards we passed noticing the commotion. A couple turn back. Then something passes through the group, a ripple, and as a unit they are on us. Two grab my arms and another my legs and lift me into the air.

I hear Macon shouting and the sirens trying to command us as I struggle. They are strong, but I manage to get a leg free and kick one. The angle is off, and I think it may have hurt me more than her. They are moving us toward the shimmer in the air. As we approach, a massive shadow crosses the window, darkening the rectangle of ocean. The sirens gasp in fear.

There is something out there—something in the ocean. We've been trying to make it back to a window and suddenly, the last thing I want to do is go through.

"Wait!" I shout. I try to twist my body out of their grip, but they hold fast. The ones who have Macon get there first, and they heave him through the window. Then it's my turn. Just before I am pushed through, I hear Odele call my name, and another, stronger voice commanding them to stop, but it's too late.

Chapter 12

I enter the ocean in a panic, thrashing until I see bubbles. Macon. He can't be far in front of me. A shadow passes above me, dark and foreboding, as I swim to him.

Something else is out here with us.

Something… wrong. And it's huge. My heart is beating so fast it's going to burst from my chest. I finally reach Macon, his eyes wild. I wrap one arm around him and my other hand covers his mouth, holding in the telltale bubbles. We start to sink. He pulls at my hand, but I shake my head.

I can't see the creature clearly. It's as if I see it through a thin membrane. Maybe another window passage. I get the impression of a diamond shape about fifteen feet across and ten feet long, with a long, blunt-ended tail. I know without a doubt that I don't want it to notice us, don't want it to know we're here.

It pauses, longer sides rippling while one end noses back and forth as if urgently searching. The movement tosses shadows over where we are. Then there's a shift in the current and the shadow disappears, taking with it my bright terror and leaving behind pure dread. I kick toward the surface.

THE SUN PRESSES on my eyes. Something on the side of my face is irritating me, digging into the skin of my cheek. A cool wind brushes across my eyelashes. I don't want to get up yet; surely it's too early. The sound of the surf surrounds me. There's salt on my lips. I am slowly waking up, prodded by my own senses. Water rushes around me soaking my legs, and then I wake fully. I'm lying on the beach. I sit up, brushing sand off my face, looking around. Where's Macon? He's a couple of yards away, lying in the sand. I call his name, scrabbling over the beach to reach his side.

"Cam?" he mumbles.

I shake him. "Wake up!"

He grabs my arms before he's fully opened his eyes, as if he thinks I am a threat. He's staring as though he doesn't recognize me. Then his face clears and he sits up, shaking his head.

"Are we…? Is this home?"

"I think so." We seem to be on the south side beach of the island. "Are you all right?"

He takes a huge breath and then laughs. "Never better." Then his expression darkens like he's just remembered something. "What was that out there, Cam?"

Before I can answer I hear my name, shouted by a voice I haven't heard in person in a very long time. On the rise is my dad.

Chapter 13

There's no moment of reunion with Dad. Anne, Macon's mother, and Ellie are with him, and once they all realize that we aren't hurt, they're just angry. It's almost funny because Dad and Anne keep asking where we've been but don't let us answer, too busy yelling at us and each other. They talk over each other: he blames Macon for taking off with his daughter while Anne says it's clearly my fault. Only Ellie remains quiet. Her face is drawn, looking as if she's balancing between fury and fear. I've never seen her look like that before. Macon tries to calm his mother, but she won't let him speak. I try to explain about the water, but Ellie stops me with a sharp look.

After much arguing and accusations, Anne walks off with Macon, taking him back to their side of the island.

I'm tired but so grateful to be back on land. As I trudge along next to Ellie and Dad, I'm surprised that he made it here so fast. He must have been closer than I thought when we talked on the phone. I ask when he arrived and what he's doing stateside, but he is in no mood for small talk with me. He grits his teeth and occasionally bursts out accusations, turning his tirade on me. He goes on about how I am "completely selfish" and "lacking discipline." I let it wash over me. I'm still a bit in a daze, the air so clean and light that it makes me heady. I greedily suck in the scent of pine. Then Dad mutters something about the island and says the word "family" with such rancor, it stops me in my tracks.

Ellie pushes me gently from behind and says, "You mother is waiting."

"Ellie—"

"Not now."

Mom is outside when we reach Windemere. She calls my name and starts toward me on the path, using her cane in an uneven clip clop run. I feel really bad then. Of course Mom would be freaking out. I went out last night and it's obviously morning now.

"I'm okay. I'm okay!" I call out as I rush to meet her so she doesn't have to travel too far.

She crushes me in her arms, which feel thinner than yesterday. "You silly, stupid girl!" She says it without any harshness, her voice thick with emotion. "Momma found your phone on the rocks. We didn't know what to think. And Macon gone too. We've been frantic. Are you all right, are you hurt?"

I try to stop the deluge of her words with my own. "Mom, I'm okay. I know it was overnight, but I am okay. I have so much to tell you." I am trying to be as reassuring as possible, but I have no effect.

Ellie ushers us all inside. Dad puts a hand on my shoulder and squeezes. I don't know if it's a hand hug and he's glad to see me or if he's just making sure I don't run off. The smell of stew coming from the stove makes my mouth water. I move toward the kitchen, but Mom seems to suddenly realize that I am soaking wet and sends me off to change. Dad is still frowning.

I think he's going a bit overboard with the angry dad bit, to be honest. He and Mom are arguing now, I can hear them from my room. I strip out of my clothes as fast as I can and pull on dry sweats and a hoodie. I need to get back out there before he upsets her. As I hurry back down the hall, I catch the end of their conversation.

"That's not the point, Serena. You can't keep control over her, she needs discipline."

"Thomas, please. This hasn't happened before. We need the whole story. Cam is a smart girl…"

"This isn't smart behavior."

"We'll talk to her." Mom sounds like she's trying to placate him. "She's not thirteen anymore. You haven't been around."

"That ends now."

Mom sits at the table, her shoulders slumped. Dad stands by the table, arms crossed. Ellie ladles stew into earthenware mugs in the kitchen. They all stop and stare at me as I come out.

"Look, I'm sorry. I didn't mean to be gone all night…" I start.

This seems to make Dad even angrier. "All night? What about the other days—didn't even take your phone. Taking off with that kid!"

"Thomas." Ellie says Dad's name with warning, her eyes fixed on him. He averts his gaze.

Then back to me: "Cam, you can't live like this. I think you should come back to town with me. Your mother can't look after you."

"What? Mom and I have been looking after each other since you left, Dad!"

"Letting you disappear with that kid is not looking after you."

"But—"

"Now that I know you're okay, I'm going back to the mainland. I think you should come with me."

I stare at him, this almost-stranger filling the house with bluster and anger. I cross my arms and shake my head. I'm not going anywhere. Dad looks as if he can't believe I'm being so stupid.

Then he says to Mom, "Not one judge will think her disappearing for days is in her best interest." He gives me an appraising look, and then walks out the door, slamming it shut.

Days? We weren't even gone two hours. We know that time passes differently in the siren world, and those two hours had felt like forever, but couldn't have been...

"You have been gone for nearly three days," says Ellie.

Chapter 14

I sip from my mug of stew, trying to process what Mom and Ellie are telling me about the last few days. I went to the rocks on Monday evening. It's now Thursday. Monday night, Jack, Macon's brother, showed up looking for Macon because he wasn't answering his phone. He and Ellie went looking for us and eventually found my phone on the rocks. Jack called his parents, and Rob and Anne joined the search. They scoured the coast and woods until late into the night. At first light, Rob and Jack took the boat out, circling the island, but found no trace of either of us.

Dad showed up yesterday afternoon. He rented a boat from Bath and came all the way to the island after he couldn't reach me. He freaked out when I wasn't here and found out that Mom wasn't sure where I was. Ellie talked him out of getting the police and Coast Guard involved. He thought Macon and I had run off together. It seems Anne had the same idea. Dad stayed last night, Mom hasn't slept much, and neither has Anne, apparently. She came to the house early this morning, begging Ellie to do something. Dad walked around the coast while Jack and Rob took out the boat again. Ellie spent the morning trying to calm Anne down and then insisted on walking with her back to her house. Dad caught up with them, and that's when they found us on the beach.

After they tell me everything, I feel terrible. I hate that I worried Mom and Ellie, and even Dad. "I'm so sorry." It's the least I can say and sounds so completely inadequate. "I didn't know. It was only an hour and a half, maybe two."

"You went to Araem?" Mom asks. She looks relieved to have me home. Behind that, I see apprehension and exhaustion.

"You went into the water again." Ellie's face is unreadable, but her cold tone and the stiffness of her spine speaks volumes.

"I didn't mean to. I had to—she took Macon."

"Who did?" Ellie watches me carefully, like what I say next could change everything.

I pause for a half-second and then just tell her. "Lyrionna."

Ellie flinches as if I've hit her. Then she stands and walks around the room in a tight circle as though she's caged here.

"Momma? What is it?" Mom's voice is calm but questioning.

Ellie lays a hand on Mom's shoulder and lets out a long breath. "She's back." Ellie sits and leans forward. "Tell me what happened."

I explain about going to the water to speak to Odele and Macon coming after me and Lyrionna grabbing him.

"That makes no sense," says Mom.

"I had to follow him, Mom."

"I understand that, but why would she take him, Momma?"

Ellie shakes her head. "Go on."

I continue, but Mom interrupts again when I talk about

Macon's trouble breathing. "Why would he have such difficulty?"

"I thought it was because he's from here," I say.

She looks to Ellie. "Dad went there with you and he was fine, right? Other people have gone there."

"There is more to Macon's story," Ellie says, then demands that I continue.

I want to grill her about Macon, but I go on to tell them about Lyrionna helping him, the quake, which makes Ellie frown, then skirt around the details of our forced exit. I'm about to tell them about the creature in the water, but Ellie interrupts this time. "What did you give her?"

"What?" I say, although I know perfectly well what she's asking me.

"Jewelry?"

"Ummm…"

"Camline." Ellie's use of my full name cuts like glass. Mom looks confused but wary.

"A promise." I hesitate, then roll up my sleeve and show her my wrist. Under the very ordinary overhead light, it just looks like a pale drawing.

"She marked you. Does she know who you are?"

"I know who she is."

"Does she know who you are?" Ellie repeats, dropping each word like stones.

"She might have guessed."

Ellie curses under her breath. I have never heard her do that before. Mom asks what's going on while she inspects my mark.

"How did she do this?" She rubs a thumb over the lines as if she can remove them. "What does it mean?" she asks Ellie.

"It means she will not forget."

ELLIE GETS up to leave shortly after we finish our stew. She seems lost in her own thoughts, not wanting to discuss my underwater trip anymore and not answering Mom's questions. I try once again to broach the subject of the creature I saw, but she stops me by saying that we all should rest. I get the feeling she's talking mostly about Mom. I offer to wash up the dishes. Mom looks very pale, and shame seeps into me, cold and deep.

"Mom, why don't you get to bed? This will be quick."

"I will. You need to sleep too, Cam. You have school in the morning."

I almost laugh. Is she seriously talking about high school right now? "Well, maybe I should take the day off?"

"No. You've missed most of the week as it is. It looks bad. I'll…" She looks around distractedly. "I'll write you a note. I need paper."

I get a notebook and pen out of my backpack hanging by the door. It feels surreal to handle these mundane items, but I give them to her. Then I remember one very important thing about me going to school—getting to William's Point.

"Where's my phone?" I need to check in on Macon anyway. Maybe his parents will keep him out of school, and I'll have an excuse to stay with Mom.

She pulls it from her pocket and slides it across the table to me. I have several missed calls: most from Dad, a few from Jack, and a couple from Blue. There are way more texts though. I don't read them yet, but tap out a quick message to Macon.

U OK? Are u going to school tmrw?

Mom finishes her note, folds it into three equal parts, and passes it to me. I peek. It says that I have been out due to family issues. I guess she isn't wrong. I check my phone again. It doesn't even look like my message was delivered. Then it hits me—Macon's phone is probably too waterlogged to be working at the moment. I don't think I've saved his landline number, but I'm pretty sure that he has called me from there at least once. I find it buried in my recent calls and click on it. It rings several times.

"Hello?" There are people talking in the background, voices raised.

"Jack? It's Cam."

"Oh, hi." He's polite, but seems as if he doesn't know what to say to me. I want to hang up.

"Um, is Macon okay?"

"He's talking to our folks."

It's not exactly an answer, but I think it's all I'm going to get from him. I go on. "Well, I'm sorry to bother you guys, but I was wondering if Macon was going to school tomorrow. I just need a ride…" A door slams in the background. "Um, if it's too much trouble, I can figure something out."

"Hang on a sec. Things are, uh…" He doesn't finish, but I can hear him put his hand over the mouthpiece and talk to someone else. Then back to me. "Okay, yeah, someone can take you, Cam. Be ready at the dock at the normal time."

I thank him and hang up. What did Macon tell his parents about where we were?

Chapter 15

I leave early the next morning and knock on Ellie's door on my way to the dock.

"How is your mother?" She stands at the doorway without inviting me in. Her hair is a mess—more than usual—and she has deep circles under her eyes. I pretend I don't notice and answer her question.

"She's okay. She went to bed early and was fine just now." Truth is she had seemed distracted, but she looked like she'd slept, at least, and had eaten breakfast with me.

"I will check on her soon."

"Ellie, I need to talk to you about when we came back. There was something in the water—something that scared me." I shiver, thinking about the fear it left in its wake.

"What was it?"

"Some kind of creature. I didn't see it very well, but it was big."

"Was it in the water? Actually in the water with you?"

I remember the impression I had about seeing it as if through something else. "I don't think it was. It was like I was looking at it through layers of glass or maybe gauze."

"But it must not have seen you."

"No. I waited until it had passed. We saw its shadow through the passageway from inside Araem. The people were terrified of it. But they threw us out to it."

She blinks. "Through the passage? While it was visible? I cannot believe she would do this." Ellie's eyes latch onto my covered wrist.

"She wasn't there at that point." I admit. "We'd kind of escaped by then. It was the others—like they blamed us."

"Not all small-minded people live on land," Ellie says wryly.

I can see Macon's boat in the distance, getting closer. "I should go."

"Camline." Ellie touches my brow and focuses on my eyes. "You must listen to me now. Do not go back in the water until I tell you it is safe. Please. Promise me." There is no command, no trying to control me, it's almost pleading.

"I won't. I promise."

This seems to satisfy her. She looks down to the dock and then back to me. "Have courage," she says nodding to the boat.

Down at the dock, Macon loops a rope around the metal cleat to hold it in place, but it's Anne at the wheel.

ANNE'S MOUTH IS A HARD, thin line as I climb aboard. Macon raises his eyebrows at me as if to warn me, even though it's completely unnecessary. He unties and pulls the rope back aboard.

"Life jacket, Cam," Anne says, as I sit.

"Right, of course." I slip my arms through the holes while gesturing to Macon to ask if he's okay. He gives me a half-hearted thumbs up. I fasten my jacket and say that I'm ready to Anne's back. She pulls away from the dock and speeds the boat toward the mainland.

"What did you tell her?" I ask Macon in a whisper.

He obviously can't hear me over the noise of the engine and wind and just shrugs. He taps his foot as if he's nervous. I can't say that I blame him. I am not sure how much Anne liked me before, but I'm getting a pretty clear picture of what she thinks of me now. I feel the need to apologize.

"Uh, Anne," I start, and Macon gives me an alarmed look like I should not be poking the bear.

It's too late, though, it's enough to start Anne off. "I think it's very clear that you've both been incredibly irresponsible. I have told Macon this, and I will be speaking again to your mother, Cam. No one knew where you were or if you were safe. And I don't suppose you'll tell me who picked you up?"

I frown at Macon in confusion, wondering what she's talking about. He gives me a "just go along with it" face.

"Nothing from you either?" Anne sounds really disappointed in me, in us both.

Spray hits my face, stings my eyes, and I have an idea. I get out of my seat and make my way to Macon's mom.

"Anne," I say, but she doesn't look at me until I touch her arm.

"You should be sitting down," she snaps. "It isn't safe."

"I will. I just wanted to say, I'm sorry. We didn't mean to scare you."

Her face softens a little. I face forward to catch more spray. The salt bites.

I lock eyes with her. "I don't want you to worry so much."

She sighs and narrows her eyes at me, but she seems less tense. Her shoulders relax a little.

"I've never been so afraid for him—not since he was a

baby," she says, and then seems surprised by the admission. "Go sit down."

When I'm seated, Macon puts his lips against my ear and whispers fiercely, "What did you do?"

"I was just trying to calm her down." I whisper back, but it comes out a little louder than I intended.

He shushes me, glancing at his mom's back, but he seems uneasy as he rolls his eyes heavenward.

WE SPEND the rest of the trip in veritable silence. Macon and I glance at each other from time to time, the air full of all we can't say in front of his mom. He doesn't even whittle the way he usually does on a boat when he's not driving.

Finally, we make it to town, and Anne lets us off telling us what time she'll be back that afternoon. "Don't be late, Macon."

He assures her that we'll both be there on time. We wave, but she doesn't leave until she sees us walking toward the school.

As soon as we're out of sight, we speak at the same time.

"What did she mean—who picked us up?"

"What was that on the boat?"

I answer first. "I was just trying to help. She was so upset."

"Yeah, she was upset! They were ballistic. My dad yelled."

"Damn." Rob is one of the calmest people I've ever met. "And, speaking of yelling fathers, that was *my* dad yesterday."

"I got that. He's a lot. Not even the scariest one in your family but definitely not my biggest fan."

I sigh. "That obviously wasn't your fault. You had no control— You couldn't help— I'm so sorry, Macon. You know, Mom was confused that you were taken there."

"We were gone for days, Cam." He looks lost.

"I know. What did you tell them?"

"I said that we went to the mainland with friends."

"Oh—but you wouldn't tell them which friends, or who picked us up."

"Well, I couldn't very well tell them that we went to a completely different world somewhere in the ocean and that time is freaky there."

I laugh. It comes out like a musical trill, and Macon's wide-eyed disbelieving look makes me laugh again.

"Not funny," he says, but he must realize the absurdity too, because he laughs hollowly.

"It actually isn't funny at all," says a pissed-off voice behind us. Blue stands there glaring at us.

Chapter 16

"What the hell is going on?" Blue's face is sharpened by her anger, and I'm afraid I read hurt on it too.

Macon and I exchange glances, we don't know how much she heard.

"You didn't even tell *me* you were taking off? I mean, you guys want to go off and be together—whatever—but I don't need your mom shouting at mine that you're missing, Macon. And you— Am I not your friend? Aren't you supposed to tell me so I can at least try to cover for you?" She interrupts her rant to take a large, pointed swig from her coffee.

I can't tell if she's madder about us being gone or just about being left out of the loop. "Sorry, Blue, we didn't mean to…"

"You didn't even text." Blue sticks her lower lip out in a comical pout, but there's an edge to it. She's still pissed off.

"Cam forgot her phone and mine got wet. Sorry. We were with friends. *Other* friends," he adds that last after Blue flashes her eyes in his direction.

She takes another sip of her coffee. "No Pumpkin Spice for you. Or you."

I raise my hands in surrender, accepting my punishment. I'm hoping that this is the end of it. We apologize, she kind of forgives us, and then life can go on like normal. Well, at least as far as she's concerned. By now, we've reached the school. People are looking at us side-long and knowingly. Macon says he'll see me later and heads to his class. Blue walks with me toward mine.

"So? Spill. At least tell me it was fun." Her curiosity peeks through her grumpiness.

"What do you mean?"

Blue pitches her voice lower as a girl from my math class passes us, staring a fraction too long at me. "You disappeared with a guy—*for days*. Didn't you…? Weren't you…? I mean, I won't judge."

As I understand what she's asking, my face goes up in flames. "No! It wasn't like that." Another person passing quickly looks away when we catch eyes. "Oh my God, that's what everyone thinks." With a sinking feeling, I realize that, of course, this is exactly what my dad thought. "How does anyone even know we were gone?"

"Small town. You forget that already?"

"Look, Blue, that wasn't what was going on. At all. I promise."

"Then where were you?"

"I—I can't explain." It is the truth.

"Why not? What 'other friends'? I know everyone you know here." She looks uncertain. "I think."

Of course she does. She probably knows everyone that Macon knows, period. Why did he have to tell her that particular lie? She's watching me closely, and I feel my cheeks heat again. I hate this. We get to the doorway of my class. Almost everyone is already inside.

"It's just complicated," I say.

"Is it? Or is it a 'different world somewhere in the ocean'?" She quotes Macon in a silly voice, as if making fun of what he said.

"What?" I try to laugh to play it off but dart my eyes around to see if anyone has heard her. Bridgette is sitting at her desk facing forward, but something about the angle of her shoulders makes me think she just turned around. I'm becoming paranoid. Or maybe not, since Blue is still staring at me.

The bell rings, but Blue doesn't move.

"We should go to class…" I say. Mr. Owens is looking in my direction. He taps his wrist as if I am not perfectly aware of the time.

"Yeah," says Blue. "See you later." I watch her spin away and am left to wonder how I'm going to smooth this over.

"Cam?" calls Mr. Owens, when I plop my backpack down on my desk. "Could you come here a minute?"

I make my way to the front of the class and behind me whispers break out like wildfire. I cut my eyes toward Bridgette as I pass her desk. She isn't talking to anyone, but she looks thoughtful, like she's trying to work out a particularly complex puzzle. The last thing I need is her thinking she knows anything about my life or my family.

Mr. Owens speaks quietly to me as if to lessen the embarrassment of being called to the front of the class. "I have a list of assignments that you missed. Have you been by the front office yet?"

I shake my head. "Was I supposed to?"

"If you have a note…?"

Oh right. "Yeah, I do. I had some family issues to deal with." I feel I need to explain.

"Just take it now and come right back to class."

The whispers cease as I turn around and for a split second,

all eyes are on me and reminding me of the ring of sirens. My classmates look at me as if I am the stranger here. I suppose I am.

Then Mr. Owens tells everyone to open our English books to page eighty-eight, and there is a general shuffling as they comply. I grab my backpack from my desk and walk out.

I GIVE my note to Miss Wren, the receptionist at the front office, telling her it was family issues that kept me from school. She arches an eyebrow at me, and I have the feeling she's heard the gossip. Fortunately, she says nothing about that as she reads the note. She pulls out a drawer in a filing cabinet and flicks her rose-tipped fingernails across folders until she reaches one that is marked "Vale, Camline." As she's tucking the note into my file, she lets me know that she'll tell my dad that I'm here.

I freeze. "My dad? What do you mean?"

She consults the pad next to her desk. "He called this morning to make sure you made it to school. I'll let him know you made it in just fine." She smiles as if she's doing me a favor.

"He doesn't have anything to do with me. He doesn't live with us." Dad isn't mentioned anywhere in my file, just Mom and Ellie.

"He doesn't?" She pulls my file out of the drawer and flips through it quickly. "I didn't realize." She seems a little flustered. "He called this morning and seemed so…"

"Full of authority?"

"Well, yes. I'm sorry, I guess I should have checked the file first."

Her pale face is suffused with pink, like she thinks she

could get in trouble. For a moment, I don't have any sympathy for her. I can't believe that she's just giving out information about me—about any student—just because a guy calls up saying he's related.

But Dad does have an air of expecting to be answered, as if it's his right. It burns me that he's checking up on me, showing up out of nowhere to suddenly play the role of my father. How does he have the nerve to snipe at Mom like she's hasn't done everything for me in the last few years? I wonder if he ever thinks about the effect he has on her. My eyes swim, pricked by angry tears.

"Is there— Do I need to let your mom know anything?" Miss Wren's voice is unsure. With my salt-touched eyes, her blonde hair glints golden under the florescent lights, her blue eyes dappled with grey.

"It's okay. Everything's okay," I say, feeling my siren power slide across with my words. Her face clears. "Could you call him back and just let him know that he should speak with Mom if he wants to know where I am? That it's school policy."

She smiles and nods, agreeing. "It *is* school policy."

"Thank you." I smile at her to drive the point home.

"Cam, you have such pretty eyes." She's still smiling as she picks up the phone, blinking slowly at me like a cat.

I hurry back down the hall, avoiding looking at anyone in the face. I feel a little bad about being angry with Miss Wren. I don't think that she meant to do anything wrong. Maybe I shouldn't have used my power on her. She probably isn't much older than our friend Jane. Still, it's better that the school takes a hard line on Dad. I scroll through my Favorites on my phone. I better warn Mom. I don't want to worry her, but it will be worse if Dad surprises her.

We're not allowed to use phones at school except during

lunch. Just as it connects, a hall monitor clears his throat at me. One glance and whatever he sees in my face brings him up short. I leave him standing in the hall and quickly tell Mom about Dad and what the school will tell him.

"I see," she says, her voice carefully neutral-sounding to me. "I didn't realize that was school policy."

"It definitely is now," I mumble, but Mom's sharp ears catches it.

"What did you do?"

"They should've checked," I say, instead of answering.

"Cam, you need to be discreet when you use your power. You can't always predict how it will take. And you never know who's watching."

"I know, Mom. I will. I do. I'm back at class now. I should go."

"Fine. Come straight home, okay?"

I assure her I will and end the call, sliding back into class. Bridgette watches me all the way back to my seat.

Chapter 17

Blue is rather quiet at lunch and seems way too focused on what Macon and I say to each other. Not that we're saying much, for that matter. I pick at my lunch. My mind is too busy with everything that's happened to pay attention to my sandwich. Macon shuts down any half-joking prying about where we have been from Luke, who fake-sulks dramatically while tearing into a burger. Diego flirts with Blue, but for once she doesn't seem into it. Wolf joins our table and is followed by Bridgette.

As they settle in next to us, Bridgette says something to Macon in French.

"Mom's doing fine," he answers.

I'm pleased that I caught the word *mère*. Macon has been trying to teach me a little French. I hate not understanding when his family, or he and Bridgette, speak it in front of me. I wonder if that's why he answered her in English.

Bridgette turns her sky-blue eyes on me. "How did the office go today, Cam?" Her slight French accent shades her question.

Despite the weird looks she's always giving me, we

generally avoid each other as much as is possible in a town
this size. So, I am instantly suspicious of a question directed
at me. I'm not the only one it surprises, I guess, because it
stops all other conversations as well.

"It was fine."

"You're not in trouble?" She takes a bite of an apple.

I wonder what her angle is. Does she think she'll embar-
rass me? Trick me into revealing something? And if so, what
does she think I have to reveal?

"No, I just gave them the note from my mom."

"That's good. You had quite an effect on Miss Wren;
didn't she, Wolf?"

I huff a laugh but feel a twinge of uneasiness. "What are
you talking about?"

Macon frowns at Bridgette, but his eyes hold questions
for me. Wolf shifts his gaze around the table, never resting on
me. He's never been completely comfortable around me.

Bridgette shrugs delicately. "She was… very complimen-
tary about you."

"What's that supposed to mean?" Macon interjects. His
question is directed at Wolf as if he has no time for Bridgette's vague innuendo.

Wolf colors under the combined attention of the table.
"She just said that she'd never noticed before how interesting
you were."

Bridgette looks annoyed that she's been cut off from
unspooling whatever tale she wanted to tell. I scoff. It sounds
ridiculous.

Luke raises his eyebrows and lets out an elongated,
"Oooooh," before Diego elbows him to get him to shut up.

"That's it?" chimes in Blue.

"Yes." Bridgette raises her chin. "She said it to everyone.
Each person that came to the office this morning." Her pretty

eyes are round and innocent as she watches me. "Every single person after you left. Isn't that funny?"

Blue rolls her eyes. "Even if it were true, how would you even know that?"

"It wasn't everyone…" Wolf says, studying the table.

"She couldn't stop talking about you while we were there." Bridgette's cheeks are flushed, which just makes her prettier.

"When were you at the office today?" asks Macon.

"We had to help out Miss Wren during third period."

"Well this settles it," says Blue, her face grave. "You are, by far, the absolute biggest ever drama queen that our school has ever produced, ever. You spend one hour filing and your takeaway is that Miss Wren is nice." She yawns and stretches as if our conversation is beyond boring and she can't possibly contain herself.

Diego laughs then, which sets off Luke. I smile like I'm in on the joke. So does Macon, but he gives me a searching look. Wolf looks embarrassed at having been involved in the discussion at all. Bridgette is unmoved. She doesn't apologize for anything. She eats the rest of her apple with quick, precise bites until the core is exposed.

AT THE END OF LUNCH, I drop the rest of my uneaten sandwich into the food scraps bin and stack my plate to the side. Macon slides up to me.

"What did you do to Miss Wren? I mean, what was that all about?" he asks, jerking his head in the direction of the table.

"I'm wondering the same thing." Blue has crept up on the other side of me.

I bug my eyes at Macon, annoyed he hadn't spotted Blue and at least warned me. Then I say mostly to Blue, "I don't know. Obviously Bridgette is… you know, doing her thing." I shrug like it's nothing.

We enter into the press of people headed to class. I have biology now and then art with Blue. They have calculus together in the opposite direction, but neither of them leaves my side. I finally stop before they walk an entire hallway out of their way.

"You know how she is when it comes to me." I appeal to Macon, hoping he'll back me up. I can't read his expression. "C'mon Blue, you said it yourself. She is kind of a drama queen."

"Yeah, I know, but Wolf doesn't usually get caught up in her shenanigans."

"He didn't though," says Macon, maybe finally remembering he's supposed to be on my side. "This is silly. We should go."

"Yeah, yeah. Oh, we have a quiz today. I forgot to tell you."

Macon groans. "See you," he says to me and then seems to change his mind. He pulls me to him and kisses me right there in the hallway. I'm so surprised, I don't even close my eyes.

I see Blue hide her face and turn as she says in mock-disgust, "Not in front of the children."

Macon then moves to my neck like he's going to kiss me there but takes the opportunity to whisper in my ear. "Talk later. Got to figure out how to keep this from her." He gives me another peck, playing up the PDA, and then whispers in my other ear, "And try not to do *that thing* to any more people."

I nod dumbly and half-wave as they walk away. Blue

complains about our bad behavior and glances back at me with narrowed eyes, even though she smiles. Macon is right, she is too shrewd and I am too bad a liar to keep brushing her off.

Maybe the answer isn't continuing to lie to her—maybe I should just tell her. Of all the people in Williams Point, she'd be the one other person I'd trust enough to tell. With her piercings, revolving hair colors, tattoo, and carefree attitude, Blue is probably the most open-minded person here. She knew the stories about Ellie and didn't seem to believe them. What would she do if she found out that some of it was true? I mull it over as I walk to class. I'm dreading seeing her again in an hour.

Chapter 18

I'm still considering the pros and cons of letting someone else in on the weird and wonderful world of what it really means to be Ellie's granddaughter when I get to art. I don't see Blue in the hallway before class, and she still hasn't arrived when Ms. Dye starts class by ringing a tiny bell. She doesn't believe in yelling; she told us so on day one. She splits us into teams because she's created a quiz-style competition to test our knowledge on artists and styles we've covered so far. The winning team gets bonus points and gets to take off the last half of class to work on our individual projects. Part of the quiz info was covered in the lecture we had on Monday. You know, the one I didn't listen to.

I'm partnered with two people I don't know well, Marie and David. Marie always brings her own pencils and brushes to class, so I'm hoping that means she'll know what she's talking about. Most of the other teams have four people on them. A couple of minutes after the bell rings, Blue and another boy I don't know well rush in. Ms. Dye barely pauses and tells them to find a group. The boy starts toward our table, but Blue pushes past him and squeezes in between Marie and me.

Ms. Dye calls out questions as hands go up around the room.

"Where were you?" I ask Blue.

"I had to stop by the office. Had to get a form." She says it nonchalantly as if there could be no other reason behind her actions.

"And?"

"And I got my form." She brandishes it with a smirk.

"Fabulous." I don't want to ask any more, but if I don't, then that will look strange. "Anything else to report?"

"Well. Not really…"

Marie frowns at me as her hand shoots up again to answer a question. Ms. Dye calls on her, but then she says that someone else in the team should answer. "How about you, Cam?"

"Uh, sorry, could you repeat the question?"

Ms. Dye purses her lips but asks it again: "What is meant by drawing something as it's seen by the eye?"

I pause and then hazard a guess. "Rendering?"

Marie's face reddens with the effort of not speaking.

"Technically, yes, but this would be representing in a way that the relationship of height, width, and depth of the subjects are taken into account."

Oh right. "Perspective." I glance at Blue.

We win. Not because of me, of course, but mostly because of Marie and David and even a few answers from Blue. Now while the rest of the class works with Ms. Dye, we get to spend the latter half of class on our projects. Blue tells Ms. Dye that we both need to do some research in the library and scores us hall passes. She drags me out of the class, shushing my feeble protests.

As Blue rushes down the hall, pulling me in her wake, I see a flash of dark glossy hair in the window of one of the classes. When I look back, there's no one there.

I tug my hand back from Blue. "What are you doing?"

"I'm getting us out of class early. Quite cleverly, I must admit."

I realize that from here, we have to pass the office to get to the library. I wonder if she has an ulterior motive. The door to the office is open, although the reception desk is empty. But then I hear my name said with such pleased joy, that I stop a second. Miss Wren is straightening up from behind one of the filing cabinets and motioning me over.

"We have passes," says Blue.

"Of course, don't worry about that." Her smile stretches across her face and shows off her even teeth. "Cam, I was hoping you would stop back by. I did speak to your father and explained our policy. He said he understood and would make the necessary changes." She says this to me as if she's confiding in me, as if we're in on something together.

"Your dad?" Blue mouths at me.

"What changes?" I ask Miss Wren.

"I—I don't know." Miss Wren looks momentarily confused. "I imagine he meant that he would speak to your mother."

"Dad?" Blue mouths again in an overblown way that makes me think she'd be yelling it under normal circumstances.

I ignore her, focusing on Miss Wren. She does seem a little overenthusiastic with me. She hasn't stopped smiling, her eyes are bright with mirth, and she leans down on her desk, as if we're all just hanging out. Her limbs are a little looser, her whole demeanor relaxed. She acts like she's a little tipsy. Or has been drugged.

I barely touched her with my power earlier. I try to remember exactly what I told her that would cause this. Ellie once said that with salt in our eyes, any land person could see something of our nature. She also said that to see that could mesmerize or enchant, even repel. Miss Wren doesn't look like she's repelled. Maybe I can fix this. My eyes are dry. It would only take a little salt water.

"You girls doing anything fun later?" Miss Wren pulls out her chair and flops into it sideways, legs dangling over the arm of the chair. "It's too nice of a day to sit inside the office. We should go out."

I do have the little bottle of sea water in my bag. I shove my hand in my bag, feeling around for it. I think Blue might notice if I got it out and splashed my face, so I am going to have to be sly. I say something unimportant about the weather as I work the little cork out of the top. Blue looks between Miss Wren and me, her face scrunching into confusion. With my hand still in the bag, I tip the bottle enough to wet my fingers and dab them against my lashes. I angle away from Blue as the salt hits my eyes.

"Miss Wren," I say, taking her hand as if I'm shaking it. I press my palm into hers to make sure I have her attention and then capture her eyes with mine. I am hyper-aware of Blue standing there, but don't dare look away. I try to sound as natural as anything, letting my siren power rise into my touched eyes. "Thank you so much for your help earlier. I'm really grateful." I really hope I'm not going to make this worse. "You did everything right and everything is back to normal now, don't you think?"

Miss Wren's smile lessens, like someone turned down the wattage. It's still polite. She takes her hand back from me and doesn't seem to know what to do with it for a second. Then she shifts suddenly, swinging her legs around to sit properly in her chair, and starts collecting papers on her desk.

"Blue, you said you had passes?" she says, as she taps the papers into order. She inspects what Blue gives her and then hands them back. "Okay you two, you better get on. Cam, I'm glad we got that worked out this morning."

"Thanks again," I say as we leave.

Blue gives me a hard look, and I know she suspects more was going on there. I try to brush it off. "Do you want to go to the library? We won't have much time to research before we have to go to last period."

"Are you kidding me right now?"

"What?" I am all innocence.

She's not buying it. "You need to explain what's going on."

I'm not proud of it, but there is a moment I contemplate looking into Blue's eyes and telling her whatever I want her to believe. It's a strong moment too. A few carefully placed words and the scrunched look will leave her face. She'll believe what I say and stop feeling that I am keeping secrets from her. We'll go back to normal.

Or, something could go wrong. I could ruin everything— lose my friend.

There's only one other thing I could do. I take a leap. "Blue, I have to tell you something."

Chapter 19

We walk out the side door heading to the library building. I slow as we approach the entrance. There will be librarians and people studying in there—not exactly the best place to tell secrets.

"Come on." I lead Blue around to the side of the library, looking for privacy, and run into a teacher I don't know. Blue holds up our passes.

"Use the main door, they're fixing the ones in back," he tells us.

We turn around. There are still too many people crossing campus, talking, goofing off. And the bell is going to ring in less than fifteen minutes, which will flood the open areas.

"Maybe we should wait until after school. It's kind of secret," I say.

"Absolutely not. You're telling whatever to me now. Let's go." She heads for the school grounds entrance.

"I'm going to get killed if I skip any more school..." But I follow her through the unguarded entrance.

"There's a sub in your history class anyway. They'll never

notice. Besides you can always have another chat with your BFF Miss Wren." Her tone is arch.

Blue takes a sharp right down a small street I don't know and then a left down an alleyway.

"Where are we going?" I think I hear steps behind us and look back, but no one is there.

"I don't want to pass my folks' shop—or the coffee shop either. Just keep up. And tell me what's going on with your dad. Or is that secret too?"

I make a face at her back but say, "He's just in town. Making trouble. Trying to be a dad, I guess."

"Well, he is."

"Trouble? Yeah, I know." I catch up to her.

She rolls her eyes. "He's your dad."

"It's not that simple. He upsets my mom." I shut my mouth. Blue knows this. We've already talked about this, at least a little. She knows it's a sore subject. It's like she's deliberately trying to antagonize me.

After a couple more turns, we come out by the road near the water. The public dock is farther up to our left, just visible in the distance. There are a few houses lining the street behind us but along the coast side are old industrial-type buildings. There's an empty boat tow parked in front of one and an old truck covered in grime in front of another. Blue powers ahead and disappears between two buildings. When I get closer, I find a nearly hidden concrete path leading out to an old dock. The scent of the ocean is so strong here, it makes my head swim. The buildings rise up high enough on each side that we are in shade until we get to the end. Stepping onto the dock, I glance over my shoulder with the sudden feeling of being watched, but the shadows don't move.

Blue has plopped herself down, feet dangling over the edge but far enough from the lapping waves that she isn't getting wet. At the sight of the water, I have a prickle of my old fear. I know now that sometimes the sea holds something even scarier than open water. The moment passes because Blue is right in front of me, waiting. Now that we're finally alone, I'm not sure how to start.

"So?" she says, acting as if nothing I'll say will be as interesting as a secret should be.

I almost smile at her attitude, but then remember why we're here and what could be at stake.

"Listen—I just have to say one thing. This isn't just about me. So, you have to promise to keep it secret."

"Cross my heart, hope to die, all that jazz."

"Seriously."

"God, Cam, don't you trust me at all?" She sounds equally pissed off and hurt.

I dive in. "Some things you have heard are true."

"So, you did shack up with Macon." She bats her eyelashes.

"No!" If only it was that simple—not that it would have been any simpler for me, anyway. My face is heating up, in part I'm sure from the first sparks of annoyance. "It's about my family."

She gestures for me to go on, her own annoyance showing.

"It's Ellie, really... She's not what she seems. She's not from here. She's... different."

"That's not news, Cam. What does it have to do with you and Macon disappearing and whatever the hell that was at the office? And why you're acting so sketchy?"

"I'm not!"

She scoffs.

I take a deep breath and count as I let it out. The salt air steadies me. "Okay, here it is: Ellie isn't... human. She's from a different world that you get to through the ocean. That's where we were, a place called Araem. And Ellie is my grandmother, so I'm like her, too."

Blue looks at me as if I've grown an extra head. Her mouth parts like she's going to say something, but then she claps a hand over it, lies back onto the dock, and begins to laugh.

"It's true."

She rolls her eyes at me and continues to giggle. Of course, she is going to require proof. There are concrete steps that lead down to the water. I roll up my sleeves and jump down to where the waves slap against the steps, plunge my arms into the water, and then splash it onto my face. My skin immediately takes on a pearly shine as the salt stings my eyes. Colors sharpen and glimmer, I think I hear a snatch of song, but then it's gone. I splash myself again and turn back to Blue.

Her laugh stops abruptly and her jaw goes slack. I know she must see my swirling eyes and iridescent skin. To me, I can see how the red and purple in her hair creates the overall magenta and can pick out the bleed from her tattoo in the surrounding skin on her arm. Her face has gone pale and her eyes are round.

"*Mon Dieu*, I knew it," says another voice, no less pretty for its shock.

Just past Blue stands Brigitte, staring at me with awe.

Crap.

We stand transfixed for a couple of seconds. I can only imagine what's going through their heads. Then Blue scrambles to her feet, and Bridgette comes a few steps closer.

"You followed us." My mind races as to how I can explain away what Bridgette must see. I know from the way her dark hair is multi-layered with sable and black and her eyes an even richer azure, that the salt has not dissipated from my own eyes. I glance down at my still-pearly arms and realize that my mark is actually glowing. To them I must look as alien as I feel, standing exposed in front of them both.

"I heard everything. I was right."

I blink my eyes and pull down my sleeves.

"How did you do that?" Blue's voice comes out in a croak.

Just then another snatch of song rises from the ocean only to disappear in a sigh. I have no idea what to say. I wanted to show myself to Blue, and in the process, let the worst possible person know my deepest secret. I search for the right words, briefly wonder if I could command Bridgette to forget but leave Blue's memories intact. My mind flits to possibilities like a confused moth around a lamp.

Then they both gasp, eyes trained past my shoulder. Bridgette leans forward. Blue rocks back as her mouth drops. I look back to find Lyrionna there.

Chapter 20

She stands in a pool of water on the dock, hair streaming down her back and sun glinting off the jewels threaded through her locks. Her dress refracts the sunlight. I am shocked to see her here, out of place and incredibly foreign. She looms over us like a painting come to life—hyper-real, mystical, and utterly terrifying.

Blue starts to speak, but Lyrionna fixes her and Bridgette with a stare.

"Be still."

The command rolls off her tongue as if an afterthought, but the effect is immediate. They both freeze in place. The sight of Blue's panicked eyes and half-open mouth tears at me. I move in front of them.

"Leave them alone. Why are you here?"

The weight of her focus moves to me, pressing against me like a solid object. I stand as straight as I can, holding myself still because I choose it, not because her command passed too close.

"Have care with your tone, child." She studies me and

then decides to tell me more. "I am here because you came to the water just now."

She can't mean when I dipped my hands in... How would she even know?

"Something changed when you visited with that land boy. He is not like these." She waves a dismissive hand toward the girls behind me. "I need you to pass a message. Tell her... Tell Ellianna the tide has not turned. The ways are not yet clear."

"What does that mean?"

But she isn't finished. "They nearly breached when you were with us." She studies my face again. I don't know what she expects to find there. "You must stay away from the water passage until I call you."

There is movement in the water. I can't see what's making it from where I stand, but Lyrionna seems to take it as a sign. She reaches forward and takes my wrist and pulls me closer. She is so strong, I can't resist. She speaks only for my ears, her voice steel silk.

"You will come to me when the mark is complete. Heed my call or face my wrath."

She presses her thumb on my wrist in the center where she marked me, and it starts to burn. I clap my hand over it, and when I lift it, see that it has changed. The tightest curl of the spiral is vein blue.

In a flash, Lyrionna is over the side and disappears under the waves.

Freed from Lyrionna's command, Bridgette and Blue have the same stunned look, the same fear-soaked expressions. I wonder if they see it reflected in my face.

"Who was that?" asks Bridgette, no trace of mocking, no malice.

"I couldn't move," whispers Blue. "What did she do to me?"

She backs away from the water without taking her eyes off the waves. Bridgette is also staring at the water, her fear seeming to turn to something akin to fascination the longer she looks.

"Let's get out of here," I say. When I touch Blue to usher her away, she jumps and puts her hands out in front of her as if to ward me off. Then, she averts her face like she's embarrassed. I don't know if it's because she was afraid of offending me, or just afraid. Whatever it is, it sits heavy in my chest.

We don't say anything until we're back at the road.

Blue shivers, rubbing her hands down her arms. "Can you do what she did?" she asks, focusing on my shoulder.

"Not like that."

"But you did something to Miss Wren." Her voice is dull.

"Blue…?" I'm almost pleading.

"It's fine. I'm fine. I have to go. I gotta get home. See you guys later." She still won't look at me properly. I don't try to stop her and watch her slip back to the path we came down earlier. I wonder if I have just lost my best friend.

"What was she?" asks Bridgette.

I forgot she was still standing here. When I look at her, she barely hesitates to return my gaze, though she seems wary. I can't believe that she was witness to all of that, can't believe that I haven't already told her to forget everything she's seen. My phone buzzes then. It's Macon wondering where I am. His phone must have dried out. I text back that I'll meet him at the public dock.

"Bridgette…"

"It's true. It's all true. I knew there was something." Her gaze drifts toward the path to the ocean. "You're like that thing from the water."

"I'm not— It's not like that."

"You are one of them, aren't you?"

I can't speak. What Lyrionna is feels a million miles away from me, but as much as I want to deny it, her blood runs through my veins.

Bridgette's face looks to be a guarded mixture of disgust and something else. It's kind of like fascination, but nothing she seems happy about. She looks me up and down and turns to leave.

"Wait." I can't just let her walk away knowing what she does.

She puts a hand up in front of her face as if shielding her eyes from the sun. "Please don't. Don't do anything—I won't tell anyone." She drops her hand, meets my gaze, and half-laughs. "We already know no one would believe me anyway."

I fight my instinct to *make sure*.

Chapter 21

At the dock, Anne is already waiting. I suppress my frustration. I was hoping to get some time to talk with Macon alone.

"Hey, sorry I missed you after school. I had to talk to Blue."

I try to surf the edge of making my words meaningful without alerting Anne that anything is wrong. He looks at me like I'm not fooling him at all. I'm dying to tell him about Lyrionna showing up, less thrilled to have to admit that both Bridgette and Blue know about her. And me.

On the trip back, Anne is civil to me and asks Macon about his day. He answers her, yelling over the noise of the boat. While they are talking, he texts me.

Where were u?

I type back: *At the water*

He looks at me sharply, but I'm still typing.

SHE showed up. We have to talk

"Ya think?" he says aloud.

"What was that, Macon?" Anne asks.

"Uh, no, nothing, Mom." He punches his thumbs on his phone to text me back.

WTF??

I shrug my shoulders, helpless to explain why. It's too hard on text.

There's more. Can u meet later?

He laughs, shaking his head and gesturing to his mom as if what I'm asking is impossible. I type back, hoping our parents will ease up over the weekend.

Tmrw?

"Maybe," he mouths the words at me.

The rest of the trip is agony trying to pretend there aren't a million things to talk about. I can also tell that Anne is still mad, even if she is calmer than she was this morning. I do feel bad about worrying her.

When we arrive at our little dock at the island, Anne cuts the engine. I'm surprised, I'd think that she'd want to get rid of me as fast as possible. Then I remember. This morning she said she was going to talk to Mom. Oh man. I probably should have warned her.

TWENTY MINUTES LATER, we're all sitting around in the living room of Windemere. I shouldn't have worried. Anne had already set this up, and Mom made tea and put out cookies as if it's a social call. Macon and I sit on two of the dining room chairs pulled up next to the couch. The tall chairs make me feel like we're on display. Anne starts by saying how unacceptable it was that we disappeared without telling anyone. Mom agrees with her but says she thinks we understand and she's sure it won't happen again. On cue, we assure them it wouldn't.

Anne doesn't want to hear our promises, apparently. She goes on to say how disappointed she is and that Macon didn't act this way when he was dating Bridgette. I'm actually stunned she says this out loud. I know Anne is good friends with Bridgette's mother, but it's such a low blow. As much as it hurts me, I can tell it really rankles Mom. She straightens as if someone pulled a string from the top of her head, and her eyes narrow. To his credit, Macon tries to shut this down, but Anne talks over him.

"It's true, Macon, that's all I am saying."

Ellie slips in at this point. Anne notices her, falters, seemingly thrown off track for a moment, but then continues. "You would have never done this before—before you got involved with Cam."

"Anne Stone, you forget yourself." Ellie's voice is quiet but cuts through the room.

"I mean no disrespect, but I'm not sure you're good for him." She says the first to Ellie and Mom and the last directly to me.

"Mom!" Macon sounds appalled.

"And I don't appreciate your husband blaming everything on my boy. He's a good kid. I don't have any trouble with him. I haven't, not until—"

"Ex." Mom speaks up, silencing Anne. "He's my ex-husband and I'm sorry he upset you, he upsets me a lot too, but I cannot and will not sit here and listen to you speak of my daughter this way." Mom doesn't raise her voice, and it's the more powerful for it.

Anne folds, putting her head in her hands. Her shoulders shake, and Macon looks at her with alarm. Ellie crosses her arms, watching her, but Mom leans forward again and lays a hand on her shoulder as if to comfort her. Anne sits up then as though suddenly taking stock of where she is. She stands, wiping her eyes, and touches Macon's cheek.

"Ever since you came to us, I have been afraid that they would take you away again."

Chapter 22

Anne recovers herself, looks at me with sadness, but doesn't apologize.

A bewildered-looking Macon whispers to me as they leave. "Tomorrow at the clearing—after lunch."

When they're gone, it's like the house takes a breath. Mom takes teacups to the kitchen and dumps the cookies back into the jar. She seems irritated and tired but all right. I pull Ellie to the side as Mom runs water in the sink.

"I saw her again." I don't have to tell her who I mean.

Ellie clutches my arm. "You promised not to go back into the water."

"I didn't go in—not really—just dipped my hands."

"Even that." She shakes her head.

"I have a message for you."

Ellie stills. It's so complete, I think again how unreal she looks in these moments. "She just said that the tide still hadn't turned and…"

"What's happening?" Mom watches us from the sink, red-checkered towel in one hand. When we don't answer right away, she continues. "Out with it. There are already too many secrets right now."

"It's *her*." Ellies sounds as if she can't believe what she's saying. Then her voice hardens. "Sending messages after all this time, and through Camline."

Mom makes a little noise of disbelief or frustration.

"She hasn't done this before?" I ask.

"Never." Ellie's mouth closes in a thin line. She goes to the living room to get the chairs.

"What was the message?" Mom asks.

"She tells me about tides as if I remember nothing, know nothing." Ellie slams a chair down at the table.

I don't want to say any more. Not if it's going to upset Ellie like this. I exchange a look with Mom.

She must see something in me because she says, "Was that it, Cam?"

Ellie focuses on me, her probing gaze almost as heavy as Lyrionna's.

"She said that they almost got through."

"Who are 'they'?" Mom asks.

"That is not possible. Cannot be possible," says Ellie.

"I had the feeling she was blaming me somehow. She said it was when we were there?" I can't keep the question out of my voice.

"Stop. What is she talking about, Momma?" Mom's face is pinched.

Before Ellie can answer, I continue. "I saw something in the water when we were coming back." Then to Ellie, "Is that what Lyrionna means? That creature—whatever it was?"

"Wait a minute. What? You didn't tell me this." Mom's confusion seems to have tipped into full-on annoyance. "Everyone sit."

We obey and head back to the living room—even Ellie. I

tell Mom about coming back to our world and the fear I'd felt seeing the shadow in the water, or through the water.

"What does this mean?" Her question is directed at Ellie.

"I am not certain. You know that we can see through to Araem from here. This world and Araem are close, and the sea is the portal. There are many passages to Araem through the water—not just around here. Anywhere there is ocean."

"Right," says Mom with a little impatience.

"Araem is not the only other realm. There is another. We called it The Underneath. It is like your stories in a book."

"A book?" I am confused by this turn.

Ellie picks up a book off the shelf, and I notice that she has chosen the Hans Christen Anderson collection I found when I first moved in here. She opens it at random.

"Here is one story. It is complete in itself." She turns to another place in the book. "This is another different story. Think of these as worlds. If I were to cut through one into another…"

She places a sharp fingernail on the page and presses. Both Mom and I exclaim, afraid she's going to tear the page. She sighs at us.

"It is only metaphor!" She closes the book with a snap and drops it onto the coffee table. "If we were to cut through, you could see into the other story—the other world. There are ways through from Araem to Earth, but those ways are closed to The Underneath. Or they should be."

"But we're seeing through to it?" I shudder.

"Sometimes this happens."

"Is this what you meant about the tides?" Mom asks.

"Exactly. There are times that the worlds come closer together—like tides bring the ocean near, or the trajectories of two planets bring them closer. It is important to stay away from the water during this time." She says this last to me with a little more force.

"That's why the sirens went quiet," I say.

"Yes, although this time has been longer. Longer than I have ever known it to be." She frowns. "And what you told me about the near breach." Ellie pauses. "What my moth—what she said to you... that has never happened in my lifetime—or hers. No one living today. There are stories—tales and warnings—about breaks in the past, long ago. The Underneath want only to conquer, to take."

"That's what the stories say?" I ask.

"Yes. There is a place in my world where the remnants of the last breach are said to be. No one lives near there now. It is sealed off so it does not affect the rest of the world. No one can go inside. The ground is dead—just dust—leached of all it had to offer. Even the air there is dry." She says the word dry like a curse.

I try to imagine a place in the siren world without the thick air or spongy ground. I did a report on the Sahara Desert once in middle school. What struck me the most is that millions of years ago, it had been the floor of the ocean. What Ellie describes sounds like that.

"But inside that wasteland, there once was a passage from The Underneath into Araem. This is why that when the tides shift—when the worlds are closer together—we do not draw attention to ourselves, we do not sing. Then the tide moves again and danger passes."

"Odele said it's been going on for years—the 'tide,' I mean. She's the girl I met, Mom, only she's not a little girl anymore. It's been months for us but years for her."

"The difference in the passage of time," Mom says.

"Yeah. Actually, that's another thing I don't understand completely."

"It is never certain. Time is not aligned with here—sometimes faster, sometimes slower, sometimes not matched at all. I do not understand why it is that way either, Camline. The worlds are on their own paths. But now, it feels very different —as if home is spinning faster than ever, or we are going slower here. Something is not in balance."

Ellie seems to turn inward for a second, then lifts her eyes to us. "The Underneath cannot be allowed to break through into Araem; if they do, they could get to this world. I do not believe there is a path direct from The Underneath to Earth. They would destroy my home first to go through."

The enormity of what Ellie is describing hits me, and I sink back onto the couch. It was already hard enough to get my head around the concept of another world, and now she's telling me there's one after that. A world that could annihilate both of ours, destroy everything. I need to know more. "What did I see? What was that?"

"Again, I cannot say for sure, but as you have described, I believe you saw a kind of forerunner—like a scout."

There's something else bothering me. "Why would Lyrionna think I had something to do with weakening the ways, then?"

"I am not positive it was you. It could have been the combination of you and Macon together."

"Why would that make a difference?"

"You are part of Araem, and part of this world. Macon is different."

"Different how? Because he's not affected by our power?"

"Yes. He is something else."

"What do you mean?" A chill sweeps across my neck raising the fine hairs. Her words ring true to me, even if I don't understand.

"Can you not see it in his eyes, in his demeanor—in his very skin?"

I think of the way that Macon seems to have a light within him when my eyes are salt-washed. I always thought that "seeing true" with him just showed how he was a good person—or reflected my feelings—but maybe there's more to it. No one else looks that way to me. With salt in my eyes when I look at the sirens, or even today with Blue and Bridgette, I can see them in a way I can't with my regular eyes, but Macon...

"So, you see him different too?" I ask them both.

Mom looks thoughtful and somewhat troubled. "I don't know, I suppose so, yes. Momma, I thought it had to do with the time he spent with you."

Ellie had taken care of Macon when he was a baby. He had been sick, and she somehow made him well. I never thought too much about why he'd been sick or how she had helped, though.

"Perhaps there is something there as well, but it is more than that."

She won't say any more.

I LIE in bed for a long time mulling over the day and what Ellie shared, questions crowding my mind. I try to text Macon again and get no response. I hope they didn't take away his phone, and I doubly hope that he's going to be able to meet me tomorrow. I have so much to tell him. I'm not sure how anything I have to say is going to go over.

"Hey babe, I spilled the beans on my secret to my hope-fully-still-best-friend and your ex—didn't go great. There's a whole other world out there that may come crashing through

the siren world and tear ours apart. Oh, and by the way, you're something that even Ellie doesn't understand."

Yeah, that should do it.

I tried texting Blue earlier. Crickets. When that failed, I tried to call her, but even her voicemail didn't pick up. Not that she's the type to listen to her voicemails, really.

I wish I'd never said anything. I wish I could take it all back. I can *tell* them not to remember. I'll just have to hope they don't spill to the entire town before I get a chance. That gives me a twinge of doubt. I just want to take it away. Walk backwards in time and erase that little bit. I probably should have filled in Mom and Ellie about that whole fiasco.

And I didn't tell them that Lyrionna has set the clock ticking for me, either.

Chapter 23

I finally make it away from the house the next day after bolting down a quick lunch. I'm glad it's Saturday. Mom spent the morning insisting that I catch up on the homework I have so that I'm not "even more behind." It feels so inconsequential right now. I don't mention anything about missing my last class yesterday. We didn't even address what I was doing near the water in the first place when Lyrionna came to me.

Lyrionna. I scratch at my wrist. The outer edges of the mark look like a white ink tattoo, pale against my skin. The inside curl is still blue, still distinctly different. I tried scrubbing it last night in the shower, but it's as indelible as if it really was sunk into my skin.

The scent of pine surrounds me as I enter the woods. The sun plays hide-and-seek with large fluffy clouds tinged with grey. Its filtered light warms my face in patches as I make my way to the clearing. My soft footsteps quicken as I get closer. I have so much to tell Macon, but also can't pretend that I'm not excited to see him. As I break through the trees, a mantle of calm falls over me. It's always eerily quiet here, and peaceful.

Right now, it's also completely empty.

Sighing, I plop down in the middle of the grass, its green scent surrounding me. I don't know how long I should wait for Macon, or if he's coming at all. I never could confirm with him. I pull out my phone to see if he's texted. Nothing from him, but I notice that my phone battery is nearly out. That's annoying.

I pocket my phone and lie back to look at the clouds, making out shapes in their depths. The trees rise up around me, green and majestic. Their tops reach high, but some of the branches are quite low. I bet I could reach them.

All of a sudden, I'm caught up with the idea of climbing one. The nearest one could work. Getting up, I go to it. I brush my hands across its bark, rough and dry under my palms. It feels alive to me, as if it's sleeping. I stretch my arms up, but I'm not quite tall enough to reach the lowest branch, even on my tippy-toes. I jump and hook my hands over the branch, pulling as I scrabble my feet against the trunk to help push me up. Within a moment, I am on the first branch, catching my balance and holding tightly as I reach for the next higher one. I make my woody way up through the needles until the branches slim, and I'm nervous to go further. Looking down, I have come higher than I thought. I'm not afraid, though, the jolt of adrenaline feels good as I mentally calculate how far the drop would be. I won't let go.

Looking out, an uneven carpet of green stretches away from and around me. My muscles burn pleasantly from the effort of climbing. I can't see our houses, or Macon's, but in the distance, I see the ever-present smudge of blue reminding me we're on an island. When I first got here, that scared me more than anything. Now I have other things to fear.

Up this high, I feel separate from the problems that wait for me on the ground. The air is lighter. A fresh breeze reaches me from the ocean, carrying salt on the wind. The quiet of the clearing nearly extends to the canopy, broken only by the soft shushing of pine needles rustling against each other. Seabirds wing past overhead, intent on their own needs and caring little of the human—*mostly human*—clinging to the branches below.

I start to make my way back down and when I am about halfway there, I hear someone crashing through the brush. I'm just about to call out to Macon, when the figure breaks through the trees. I freeze, mouth open, shout caught in my throat. It isn't Macon at all, but his mom.

Anne's face is flushed, and she mutters to herself as she stomps into the middle of the clearing. Once there, she raises her face to the sky and lets out a frustrated-sounding yell. It surprises me so much that my foot slips. I find my balance again and hug the tree to me, feeling my heart pound into its trunk.

Anne's face is twisted in anger. "I have kept him safe just as I promised! Why can't you help me protect him?"

For a split-second, I think she's screaming at me, but she's turning in a circle like she's holding the trees, or the very sky, to account. Maybe it's fear I see in her face—maybe anger stoked by fear. Whatever it is, this is not right. Anne is cool and calm, a little prickly maybe, but not one to be shouting at the heavens. Although lately, I have seen a side of her that is not at all as level-headed as I'd come to expect. She kicks at the ground and then rushes to a tree across from where I am hidden, disappearing from my sight. From the dull thumping, it sounds as if she is battering her hands against the trunk.

After a moment, she stumbles back into the clearing and,

like she can no longer hold it up, bows her head. Her shoulders shake.

"I don't know how to do this. What do I do?"

Her voice is quiet, but it's loud enough to reach me where I am. *I* don't know what to do. It isn't like she would take comfort from me, and something tells me that she'd be angry with me that I had seen any of this. I'm still contemplating when she straightens and puts herself back together. She dusts her hands off on her jeans and then smooths them over her hair. She wipes her eyes and takes a deep breath. When she leaves, she goes west toward our side of the island.

Chapter 24

As soon as I am sure she's gone, I scramble down out of the tree as fast as I can, dropping to the ground with a grunt. I pull out my phone and click on Mom's number, but my phone dies without connecting. Crap. I don't know if I should go after Anne, try to outflank her, and get home before she reaches Mom and Ellie. Or I could go find Macon. But maybe he's out on the boat with his dad and brother. I stand motionless for a second. Warning Mom is probably the best thing to do right now. Then at least I'll be there if... If what? Hell, I have no idea why Anne is going there.

I'm picking my way back to the main path and trying to visualize the best route back to avoid running into Anne when I hear my name. Macon jogs toward me up the path that leads to his side of the island. His dog Beau zigzags along next to him.

"Hey, sorry I'm late. My Mom was all over me this morning, but she's out for a walk now." He is out of breath as if he ran the whole way here. His flushed face and panting remind me uncomfortably of when we were in Lyrionna's cave.

"She went that way," I say jerking my head west.

He looks confused. "I thought she was heading to the south beach. You saw her?" His eyebrows lower over his wide eyes. I can almost see the thoughts run around his mind at what that could mean.

"She didn't see me."

His face clears. "Probably for the best. She's in some kind of mood."

"I noticed." Beau wriggles his body next to my leg, and I give him a scratch behind his ears. "Thought I'd try to get back before her to warn the others. Or at least call, but my phone's dead. Can I use yours?"

"They'll be all right," Macon says, taking my hand and tugging me back toward the clearing. "Miss Ellie can hold her own, and I'm pretty sure your Mom can too."

My feet drag, but his hand is warm. I want to be convinced, so I don't put up much of a fight, letting him lead me. I don't even know what I'd tell Mom, and I probably couldn't outrun Anne the way she was walking anyway. Plus, who knows when Macon and I will be able to be able talk alone again—be alone again. My cheeks warm at that, then I mentally chide myself. There's too much going on for us to...

Macon pulls me into his arms. His mouth is on mine, and that's all I can think about. My arms snake around his back as he pulls me closer. I feel the gentle dips and ridges of his spine under my fingertips and his quickening heartbeat near mine. His hair brushes my forehead, and his hands shape my waist. The scent of pine is strong, like I've just crushed needles in my hand. Salt is on our lips. I am suspended—as if I were back in the tree and let go, only to float up instead of falling.

With great effort, I shift my palms to press against his chest and gently move my head back. My breath is ragged, as though I was only breathing properly in his embrace. His is the same, and he has high spots of color in his cheeks. The light around us is buttery, the air still, soft and dreamlike.

"Wow. I missed you." He sighs and licks his lips.

My eyes snag on the movement, but he steps back, still holding my waist. I am so very conscious of his hands, our mingled breath, and the drum of his heart under my palm. I could very easily fall back into the undertow of his kiss.

Then Beau barks. It's enough to remind me that there's a million things we need to catch up on. Beau barks again and growls, the fur around his ruff rising. A spike of fear jolts me, as I wonder what it can be now. I follow his gaze to the tree line, but there's nothing there. The silly dog is barking at a tree.

"Hey bud, that's enough." Beau looks up to him, his sad doggy eyes worried. Then he's back to barking at the tree. "Beau! Come on, boy." Macon pats him on the back, and Beau leans into his touch.

I focus on the tree that has Beau's attention. Its rough bark has lines and fissures through it as if it had gotten too large for itself and cracked. It's an older tree, I guess, because it's tall—even taller than the one I was in. I look round to find the tree I climbed. It's almost directly across the clearing. I think this is where Anne had come. I think this might be the tree that she was banging against. While I am puzzling that out, Macon is speaking softly to Beau, calming him.

I'm drawn to the tree. I can't stop myself from walking right up to it. I lay my palm against its trunk and, just as with the other one, get the distinct impression that the tree is alive. Of course it's alive, I know it's a living tree. But this one feels *alive*—like it's going to shift or move right under my hand.

Macon joins me, but Beau hangs back, a little whine escaping his muzzle.

"What are you doing?"

"Feel this." I want Macon to feel what I do, the life-force inside the tree.

The moment he touches the trunk, he freezes, tightening up as if he's touched a live wire.

"Macon?"

I pull his wrist. It's stuck fast. I can feel the muscles corded underneath his skin. I'm finally able to shift his hand. A sound rushes out of his mouth, and he collapses to the needle-strewn forest floor.

Chapter 25

I pull Macon away from the tree. His still body is too much for my arms, so I brace my legs and use my own weight to shift him. My brain is rushing, stupid facts bubbling up. When someone is passed out, they call it deadweight because the person can't help you move them. I won't think about that phrase. His chest is rising and falling, so I'm just being ridiculous. Beau whines. My thoughts jumble like broken toys, nothing staying still long enough for me to hold them together. All I can think is that I have to move him away from the tree. He's taller than me and outweighs me, but I am strong. And super motivated.

I drag him back all the way into the intermittent sunshine of the clearing. I give him a little shake and call his name. His eyes move under his lids, but he doesn't open them. Beau paces around us, sniffing at Macon and whining.

I can't remember what I've read or seen on TV—what you're supposed to do for people like this. Mom never passed out on me. I lift his head into my lap and brush his hair back from his forehead. He looks younger with his closed eyes and quiet expression.

I want to call Ellie. She would know what to do. But Ellie doesn't have anything as perfectly normal as a cell phone. And my cell is dead. I feel Macon's jacket pockets for his phone. I could call Mom, but Anne is probably still there. His phone isn't in his jacket. It must be in his back pocket where it'll be hard to reach.

Maybe Anne is on her way back and will stumble into this clearing, finding me holding her unconscious son. She's going to kill me. As I look into his perfect, yet still, face, I know it's quite possible I am no good for Macon. She may be right about me, after all. I trace my knuckles across his cheek. He starts to glow from within and I realize that my eyes have filled with tears.

Siren commands mean nothing to him, but what about our song? Ellie sings to the animal skins she treats to "wake them," she said. I could try. It helped Mom. Ellie's complicated melody begins at the back of my throat, and I bring it forward into a soft hum. I stroke Macon's face and sing to him, willing him to wake. Beau crouches near us, close but wary, his whole body focused on the boy I hold. The song fills the clearing, but doesn't seem to touch Macon.

I stop humming.

I am going to have to move him, get to his phone, and call someone. A hot tear slips down my cheek and as I wipe it away, I look up. The trees shimmer in my eyes as if they are moving. A breeze blows through them, but I don't feel it where I am. It shakes the pine needles sending whispers through the branches. They swim in my vision, winnowing down to a glow that comes from within the heart of the tree that Macon touched. I blink; it fades.

When I look down, Macon stares up at me with his hazel eyes.

"Are you crying?"

"Are you okay?"

Our questions overlap each other. I strangle a laugh, relived to see him scowl.

"What happened?" He sits up and runs a hand through his hair. "I'm dreaming."

"You're not. You just fainted."

"I— No. What?" He gets to his feet and shakes himself like Beau after a bath. "We were looking at the trees." He stumbles a little and Beau barks.

I stand and take his arm. "Maybe you should sit back down, Macon." He sways a little.

"Yeah, all right, fine." He eases himself to the ground.

I sit with him. Beau whines. I try to pat him, but he shimmies away from my touch and seeks out Macon's. Macon strokes him, and the dog snuggles closer.

Macon is staring at the trees. "I don't get it." His voice is soft.

"It was weird." My heart is slowly coming back to a normal rhythm. "What happened?"

"I don't know. We were standing by the tree, and now we're back in the clearing."

"I pulled you back here."

He frowns and looks away from me; his cheeks go pink.

"Are you sure you're okay?"

"Yeah. I'm fine. Never mind. Just… You should tell me about Lyrionna." A shudder runs through his body, and he swallows.

My hand goes to my wrist. There's so much we need to talk about. A cloud crosses the sun, leaving us in shadow and acting like some kind of bad omen.

"She came to me by the water to deliver a message for Ellie."

Before I can continue, he asks me, "Where was this? Where were you after school yesterday?"

He's waiting for an answer, so I tell him the truth. "I went down by an old dock near some industrial-type buildings."

"With Blue?"

"Yeah, how did you know?"

"Wolf saw you leave."

"Oh." I briefly wonder if that's how Bridgette knew to follow us.

"Hang on—" Realization seems to dawn on him. "*Blue* was there when Lyrionna showed up?" I hear the horror in his voice.

"Well, yeah." I shift, wondering how mad he's going to be.

He's waiting, barely breathing, for the rest of it. I decide I'll rip off the proverbial Band-Aid. "I told her. I told Blue. Right before."

His mouth drops. "You're joking. What did she say?"

Might as well drop the other bombshell as well. "Bridgette was there too."

"What?" He surges to his feet. Beau leaps up with him, tail wagging. Macon's voice cracks the serenity of the clearing. "What were you thinking?"

His tone is so accusatory my anger trips. I know in some distant part of my mind that I'm still frightened and I'm mad at the situation, which is pretty much my own fault. It still doesn't stop me from snapping at him.

"I didn't mean for it to happen! She followed us. Then flipping Lyrionna showed up and commanded both of them, and now Blue thinks I'm some sort of freak of nature."

"And Bridgette?"

"I don't care what she thinks," I mumble, my anger melting away into regret. "Blue was getting suspicious. I didn't want to keep lying to her." I'm trying to justify it—half to Macon and half to myself. "Anyway, it was a mistake. But it's going to be okay, though, I'm going to take care of it."

"What do you mean?" Macon narrows his eyes at me, mouth settling into a hard line. Then as if realizing what I'm getting at, he shakes his head. "You can't."

"I actually can. They aren't immune."

"Cam, it isn't right. It isn't fair. And I don't even think you fully understand how to use it."

I know what he's saying makes sense but... "You didn't see her. Blue was really upset, Macon. She's not answering any of my texts. What other choice do I have?"

"I don't know. But if you do this, she won't trust you."

Unless I make her trust me.

The unbidden thought comes so swiftly that it scares me. I try to quash even the idea and ignore Macon's expression. I never asked for this power, but I have it. Am I supposed to just pretend I don't? Okay, I probably shouldn't go as far as *making* her not be afraid of me. But if Blue could just forget what happened by the water—if Bridgette hadn't been poking her nose into my business. She said she wouldn't say anything, but why should I believe her? This is the simplest solution.

"There's more," I say, instead of giving voice to my doubts. "Ellie also told me and Mom some things."

He doesn't look convinced that we're done talking about our friends, but he listens, eyebrows set in concentration mode.

"There's more than just the siren world. There's something—*somewhere*—else. They call it The Underneath. The creature we saw in the water is from there. I think it was hunting—testing for cracks in the defenses. It may have found some, and we may have helped start it."

"Us? Like our world?"

"You and I."

"The earthquake?" He asks, as if what I'm suggesting is ridiculous.

"Maybe? Something is different there already, we just might have made it worse."

I explain about the tide theory and the length of the most recent event.

"That's why Odele looks so much older."

I nod. "And Ellie thinks that if The Underneath gets through to Araem, they could come here, to Earth."

"Damn. But that doesn't explain what we had to do with all this. Maybe it was just wrong place, wrong time for us—bad timing."

"It might not be so simple." I gesture to the clearing. "What if this has something to do with it?"

"Here?" He gives me a quizzical look.

"Macon, there's something special about this clearing. I felt it the first time I came here. You told me yourself…"

"It is special. But I don't see…" He trails off, walking directly toward the tree he'd touched before.

"Hang on— I don't think that's a good idea." I run in front of him blocking his way. "That tree made you fall over. Don't touch it again until we know more."

"It doesn't make any sense that a tree could do that. It's not possible."

I laugh, full-throated and bordering on hysterical. "Were you or were you not the guy with me in an alternate world like five minutes ago?"

"Okay. Yeah. But you think the clearing might have something to do with the earthquakes? Nothing bad happens here. And how could a tree make me faint? I come here all the time. It's like home." The last is almost to himself. Then he lifts his head. "I can hear something. There's something there."

I don't know if I'm brave enough to touch the tree myself at this point, but as Macon advances again, I back up, keeping myself in front of it. "You really scared me. Please don't."

He stops. "I scared you? I guess that's a change."

"Huh?"

"Cam, jumping in the water? Going to see Odele alone? That kind of thing freaks me the hell out."

"I didn't mean to..."

"I know. And we can't control what others do. No matter how much we care about them."

The breeze lifts again to my right, coming out of nowhere. It doesn't behave as a breeze should, sweeping in from one direction and then away in another. Instead it seems to move in a circular pattern through the trees around the clearing, passing from tree to tree like "the wave" at a football game. Pine needles rustle and branches sway. Macon tilts his head as if he's listening to something far away. His eyes lose focus, and he cants his ear toward the movement of the wind. Beau barks, and in the split second I look to the dog, Macon slips past me.

"Wait..."

"It's all right, Cam..." He reaches the tree just as the wind circle completes and takes up residence in its branches. As they sway, Macon places his hand again on the trunk. I'm a second behind, slapping my hand over his. In the shushing of the needles moving against each other, I swear I hear it whisper his name.

∾

THE WIND DROPS SUDDENLY, and Beau barks again. Macon is still upright and besides a look of pure wonder on his face, he seems okay. I tug his hand to get him to step away with me. He seems reluctant to remove his hand from the bark, but after a moment, he comes with me. I breathe a sigh as the sun peeks out and warms my skin.

I peer at him, running my hands from his shoulders to his wrists. He interlaces his fingers with mine.

"That was amazing." He lets go of my hands and wraps his arms around my waist. He actually lifts me off the ground and spins me in a circle. His face is lit with joy.

"What happened?" I ask when he finally sets me down.

"I *heard* the tree."

"You what? That's not possible…" I trail off as he grins at me.

"Tell me what's not possible, siren girl," he says, bringing up my own argument.

He literally dances around me. Beau thinks it's a game and jumps around with him. When it looks as if Macon is going to pick me up again, I twist out of his grasp.

"Hang on!" In spite of my confusion, I find myself smiling. His joy is so beautiful to see. "Just tell me what's going on."

Instead, he kisses me. It's a kiss full of jubilation, of pure happiness. He tastes like sunshine. Again, I am floating, this time buoyed by his delight. When we break, I am once again breathless. His lips are reddened from kissing me, his eyes bright as lanterns. He leans back toward me, but somehow, I'm able to resist the pull of the oblivion of his kiss.

"Macon, wait. Talk to me, please."

He touches my hair and then glances back at the tree line with a faraway look. "It was like remembering a dream I knew I'd had. It was *right*. Like belonging." He looks back to me and says, "I could hear the voice of the forest. Like it was talking to me."

His happiness is so apparent that I don't even need salt in my eyes to see his innate glow. My brain skitters over that, and I feel I'm forgetting something.

"I've never felt like that before—not in my whole life."

His whole life. That phrase echoes in my brain. In the midst of his joy and the strangeness of the moment, I think of something else Ellie brought up. "Macon, this might sound weird, but I think we need to talk to your Mom. We need to ask her about your adoption."

I tell him what Ellie said. He's quiet at first and then pushes back. He says staunchly, as he has before, that his parents are his parents, Jack is his brother.

"Of course they are, Macon, but you had to come from somewhere. I think the clearing feels so important to you for a reason, and your Mom may know why." I take a breath. "When she was here earlier, she was yelling at it."

"What do you mean?"

"She was shouting about protecting you."

He lifts his eyebrows, pushes out a breath, and then stares into the trees.

I go on. "And you can't think that what just happened is normal."

"I don't even know what normal is anymore."

"Yeah, maybe we have to adjust what that means."

He flicks his eyes toward me and then stares back at the trees. "Regardless, you said that Ellie was certain of one thing. We can't let The Underneath break through—to Araem or Earth." His eyes reflect my own worry. "If what she thinks is true, that we had something to do with that earthquake or whatever, maybe we can help fix it?"

"Okay, but how? We need to know more."

"Maybe *it* could help?"

I don't know what he means at first, but then he's heading back toward the tree. I follow after him, biting back another warning. He pauses only for a second before he reaches out to the tree again, laying his hands on the trunk. I hold my breath, not sure what will happen. After a moment, he drops his hands.

"It's gone. I can't hear it."

The desolation in his voice makes me want to wrap my arms around him. He leans forward and rests his head against the tree.

"Can you still feel it, though?"

He raises his palm to the trunk. "I think so."

I move my hand next to his on the bark, my pinky touching his.

"Cam, there is something unique about this tree. It feels alive, like *alive* alive."

"I felt that too."

He pulls me close and slips one arm around me and the other around the tree trunk in a sort of group hug. As my cheek presses against the rough bark, I almost laugh at us, but strangely it feels right. It feels good. He closes his eyes, but I watch him. Deep within the tree, I feel something like a sigh.

I blink and when I open my eyes, Macon is staring at me.

"Okay, let's go talk to my Mom."

Chapter 26

Macon is quiet as we walk. He absently pats Beau, who wants to stay close to him. I feel the same way, holding Macon's hand and wondering what we're going to say to Anne when we get there. I don't know what to expect. What I definitely don't expect is to see Rob waiting on the path, as if he knew we were coming.

"Dad? What's going on?"

"Mail for Serena, and I'm picking up your mother."

"Where's Mom?" Macon swivels his head looking between my house and Ellie's cottage.

"All up at Windemere."

"Good. I want to talk to you both."

If Rob is bothered by Macon's tone, he doesn't show it. I squeeze Macon's hand.

As we walk in, I take quick stock of the scene. Ellie stands by the cold fireplace, inscrutable as ever, but Mom looks troubled, a letter on the table before her. Anne sits at the table as well; she seems surprised that Macon is here. The air in the room is charged. Beau lets out a small whine and plops down by Macon. I'm not sure what we've walked into.

"Cam, you're back, good. I need to speak to you." Mom fidgets with the letter.

"And we should get back," says Anne, rising, with a hard look at Macon. "You're supposed to be fixing nets."

"I'm finished. I need to talk to you and Dad."

"It can wait. We can talk on the way home." She glances at Ellie and Mom. "We won't take up any more of your time. I think we're clear here."

"I would not be so sure, Anne Stone." Ellie focuses on me. Her eyes drift across my wrist.

"Well, I am clear. Macon and Cam, I won't tolerate this anymore. No more sneaking off, no more running around."

"Hang on, Mom." Macon's voice is firm.

Rob touches her arm and murmurs something, but she bats his hand away. "No, I'm serious. Don't tell me to calm down."

"Perhaps, I should tell you to calm down," Ellie says mildly, almost to herself.

"No." Macon shoots her a look. Then says to his mom, "This is important. I need to know where I came from."

Anne sucks in a breath, and a muscle twitches near her eye. No one moves for a good three seconds.

"No, son, this is not a public discussion," Rob says into the silence. "Let's go."

His voice is even and calm but effective. Anne glances once to Ellie then walks out the door. Rob nods to Ellie and Mom and herds Macon out after Anne, Beau on his heels. Macon mouths, "See you" to me. I try to give him an encouraging smile but don't say anything until the door has closed behind them.

"I need to—" I start, but Mom interrupts.

"Cam, sit down," Mom says to me.

I pull out a chair and really look at Mom for the first time since I came back. The lines around her mouth have deepened and she has circles under her eyes. Her face is drawn, and I notice the strain she's carrying in her shoulders.

She continues. "I need you to be calm and listen."

I glance at Ellie, but her expression gives nothing away.

"Did Anne say something?"

Mom gives an impatient cutting off motion as if Anne is the least of her worries.

"What is it?" My mouth goes dry.

Her fingers play over the letter. "Your dad— He wants custody."

"What?" That is the last thing I expected her to say. "Why?" It's almost laughable.

"He doesn't think I am the best parent for you—especially after what he calls 'your disappearance.'" She sounds sad, almost resigned.

Rage fills my head, stopping up my ears and coloring my vision. I fumble for my phone. I'm going to take care of this right now. There's no way he can waltz back into our world after abandoning us and say he's the better parent. It'll push Mom back over the edge. She'll get sick again. Everything we achieved by bringing her here could just evaporate.

Mom's talking to me, but I can't hear her, can't focus on anything except the white-hot fury coursing through my veins. My breath is a struggle, and my hands are shaking so hard that I jab ineffectually at the power button before remembering that my phone is dead.

"Camline!" Mom snatches my phone away from me and catches my hand. "Look at me."

I focus on her then, my breath still fast. She looks worried.

"It's okay, Mom, I'll handle it." I manage to say, wanting to smooth the lines on her face.

"No, you won't. Unless…" She pauses as if uncertain.

"What?"

"Unless, you want to try living with your dad for a while."

I am floored. "Wh—why?" I splutter.

"You don't have to decide anything now, but it might be a chance for you to reconnect with him. Not live on an island, maybe? You have a say in this too."

"I can't believe you'd even suggest that! This is my home now. I will handle this right now." I reach for my phone again.

Something changes in her expression. "I said no." Her voice gains a little strength. "You aren't handling this. I'm the Mom here. Just… take a minute. Why don't you go take a shower and calm down?"

She won't give my phone back until I do as she asks. I'm still fuming when I step under the spray, but as the hot water rushes over me, my heart starts to calm. I breathe in and out in counts of four until the roaring in my ears dulls. All I can think is why now? Why is Dad here now when he was blatantly uninterested in me for the last few years?

My wrist begins to burn, and I almost cry out with the shock of it. Another curl of the spiral pulses and then settles into blue. The water beats down over my head as I stare at it. I stifle a hysterical laugh. I have bigger fish to fry.

Chapter 27

I choose a long-sleeved T-shirt, even though it's probably a little too warm for it, so I can cover the changing mark. I don't want to worry Mom with anything else right now. I'll talk to Ellie about it. Maybe she can help me understand what it means. But she's already left by the time I come out of my room.

I haven't told either of them about what happened in the clearing, but I'm pretty sure that can hold off until Macon and I know more.

I set the table while Mom grills me about the homework I did earlier. I assure her that I'm caught up. All I want to talk about is Dad's dumb request, but Mom still looks tired. She's even using her cane inside, so I don't push it.

We don't say much as we eat. Mom smiles at me every time she catches my eye. One or two even seem sincere. I scratch at my wrist but force my hand down when she frowns at it.

"Is that a new batch of Ellie's sea salt?" I ask, trying to distract her.

"Yes, we made it the other day." She pushes the bowl closer to me with another smile.

"Thanks." I sprinkle fat flakes of salt over my vegetables. Then I concentrate on finishing my meal and try not to think about Dad.

After dinner, we clean up together. I said I'd do it, but it's like she has something to prove. I wash dishes as she puts away leftovers. When we're done, she finally gives my phone back to me and goes off to have a bath.

I plug it in and message Macon as soon as it powers up: *Any news?*

I wait impatiently, hoping that he hasn't had his phone taken away. After a moment, my phone buzzes.

Super vague. All she says is that it was closed.

I assume he means a closed adoption, meaning that there might not be any information about Macon's birth parents. My phone buzzes again.

Didn't mention the other stuff

It's probably best not to discuss talking trees at this point. I text him again: ***Internet?***

He writes back: ***Already looked. Not much there***

Then it hits me. We actually have a secret weapon in this area—a friend who knows all about research and would keep it on the down low if we asked her.

I message Jane in California, asking her for a favor. She types back almost immediately with lots of exclamation points. I give her the details I have, and she agrees. Knowing she's on the case feels like some progress.

Still nothing from Blue. I check her social media, but she hasn't posted anything since Friday morning. I check the coffee shop page, but they are just hammering on about Pumpkin Spice being In Stock!

I lie back on the bed. I type out another message to Blue but don't hit Send.

I FIND myself in the clearing again. A whirlwind blows around me. It funnels the smell of pine and salt into my face until I am giddy with it. My hair flies around my face blocking my vision and then letting me see, like a strobe light. I see Macon in snapshots. He's standing by the tree from earlier, knocking on the trunk. It's like a stop motion film. Then the bark of the tree swings open like a door and Macon steps inside. He throws one last look over his shoulder to me before he disappears. I run after him, but the bark has sealed closed and there is no trace of him. I call his name and bang my hands against the trunk until my hands are bloody.

The whirlwind increases until it fills my ears and pulls me away from the trees and right up into the sky. I turn and turn and turn until I am dizzy and sick. I am far away from the clearing now, far from the island, suspended over the deep blue ocean. Then it suddenly stops. I hang in the air for a second, like a cartoon character, and then drop. As the ocean rushes up toward me, it parts and Lyrionna stands with her arms open and teeth bared, ready to catch me.

I GASP AWAKE before her chilly hands reach me. My heart hammers in my chest and cold sweat slicks my body. I sit up pushing off the covers, feeling nauseous, as if I'm still spinning.

My light is out. Mom must have done that, because I don't

remember even getting ready for bed. Once the room stops moving, I pad quietly as I can to the kitchen to get a glass of water. Burning pain lances across my wrist, and I nearly drop the glass. Another swirl of the spiral colors in as I watch.

My time is running out.

Chapter 28

I sleep fitfully and am up by the time dawn breaks. Too restless to sit in the quiet house and not wanting to wake Mom, I dress silently and slip out the front door. I walk down to Ellie's, but even her windows are still covered.

I head down toward the slice of beach where Ellie first showed me the sirens, where I saw through to their world and learned what I was. It feels so long ago now. I feel like a different person. Back then, I could barely manage to step onto the sand, had to force myself to walk into the surf. Now I hang back because there really could be monsters in the waves.

Correction: there are definitely monsters out there.

I tap my pocket for my phone, but I've left it charging on my bedside table. I'm curious to see if Macon or Jane have texted me back but decide not to go back for it. I don't want to risk waking Mom. I'm pretty sure I can live without the phone for a bit—despite what everyone seems to think about my generation.

Somehow, I did pick up the wooden seahorse Macon carved for me. I run my thumb over the whorl of its tail, and stare at the waves coming in, listening to the sigh of the surf. It is mesmerizing and comforting. I watch the rhythmic motion of the water pulling out and crashing back until it gradually dawns on me that I'm hearing something else mixed in: a motor—someone is coming.

It must be Macon, but I'm surprised he'd be able to sneak away this early and not sure why he'd come by boat. I make my way back up the beach and head over to the dock. The boat isn't coming from Macon's side of the island but from the direction of the mainland. I squint into the distance trying to make out who's driving. It better not be Dad. I might completely lose it with him if it is.

But it turns out to be worse than that. The boat pulls up to the dock, bumpers hitting the edge, with Bridgette at the helm.

My mind races, and I can't even form the words to ask her what she's doing here as she ties up her boat. She climbs out, warily watching me as if she has to be prepared in case I do something.

We stand across from each other, only yards apart. Finally, I find my voice. "What do you want?"

"The truth." Her chin is lifted in what I assume is defiance, her eyes challenging, but I sense the fear behind them.

I laugh. "What do you expect me to say?"

"You'll probably lie just as you have all along."

"That's what you really think? I've never told you a lie, Bridgette."

"But you lie to everyone. You're lying to Macon."

"I don't have to justify myself to you, but so we're clear, Macon already knows about me."

She darts her eyes away for a second, as if contemplating whether to believe me. Her pretty mouth turns downward and her nose wrinkles.

"You don't want the truth from me, Bridgette. You want me to tell you that everything is fine. That you imagined what you saw with Blue."

She studies my feet. "That might be worse."

It seems hard for her to admit. She doesn't sound certain, though.

I try to imagine what it would be like to be able forget about Lyrionna, about the helpless feeling of being in a siren thrall. If someone offered me the same, would I accept? But I know I can't even entertain the idea. It's not possible for me. It's inside me—stamped in my bones, written in my very blood. I can never forget. But Bridgette doesn't have to remember.

"I could do that for you," I say, wondering why I am making the offer instead of just doing it. Macon's concerns come back to me, but what do I care if Bridgette trusts me? She wouldn't even remember. And if I can get to Blue too, then I'd just hit the reset button on all of this.

Bridgette regards me through slitted eyes. "I just want to know one thing—the truth about one thing."

I cry out with pain. It's sharp and sudden, surprising me. My wrist is on fire—more intense, worse than before. I watch in horrified fascination as the last curl of the spiral burns blue and settles.

The mark is complete.

"Bridgette, you have to go." I try to keep my voice level, but that's hard when you're trying to talk past gritted teeth. The pain has faded but fear has crawled into my belly.

She is frozen, eyes on my wrist, body tense. I hear a splash.

"Go now!"

I try to bodily push her toward her boat, but she resists me. She plants her feet and pushes back against me, her hands small but strong, eyes flashing with the supposed indignity of me touching her. Behind me I hear another splash. Bridgette's face falls and her eyes go round with shock. I turn to find two copper-haired guards climbing onto the dock. Their green-tinged skin shines unreal in the morning sunlight. I think they are the same ones that were with Macon and me, Kerin and Kiyash. Their expressions are set, eyes dark pools.

"You have been called," one says to me. The gravelly voice is Kerin's.

"I just need to…" I start to say, but he clamps his hand on my wrist.

"There is no time. We must go." He pulls me toward him.

As I peel away from her, Bridgette's push turns into a grab. I don't know what's going through her mind, if she's trying to help me or it's just instinct, but she doesn't let go.

We are pulled off the dock together and are suddenly under the water turning and moving. I try to disentangle her fingers from my shirt, but she will not let go. Bubbles stream out of her open mouth, and her eyes lose focus as they fill with water. My vision is enhanced from the sea water, so everything is in sharp detail. The other guard, Kiyash, looks confused. He places his hands on Bridgette's arms. I can't tell if he's trying to get her away from us or take her with us.

Then a blast crashes through the water. My wrist aches as Kerin holds on tighter so we aren't separated. Bridgette is shaken loose from me, but Kiyash holds her, keeping close to us. The guards press on, shooting through the water with us. As another underwater *boom* hits, we tumble into Araem.

Chapter 29

We land on cushioned ground, tangled together and dripping wet. Bridgette pushes away from me, spitting water, and springs to her feet like a cat. I stand as well. I'm on high alert, adrenaline spiking in my veins. Bridgette looks as if she may leap out of her own skin. She's trying to look everywhere at once, head turning and eyes rolling. My breath is tight, and hers comes in small gasps.

We are in a grove of filigree trees. Their pastel-colored fronds waft slowly in the unseen currents in the air here and create a screen around us. Strange, deep red, segmented flower-like plants grow around the bases. The guards flank us on each side but have released their holds. I'm not paying attention to them anymore.

Lyrionna stands in front of us, imperious and scary as ever. Her presence is so powerful, she seems to tower above us. She examines me and then turns to Bridgette.

"Why did you bring this one to me?" She addresses the guards without looking away from Bridgette.

"She held fast and there was no time to tarry," says Kiyash.

Lyrionna seems to accept this explanation, although she doesn't appear to be happy about it. "I felt the blasts." She focuses on something behind us, runs a hand through the air as if closing a curtain and very quietly, so I almost miss it, sings a short snatch of song. The shimmer of the large window disappears as if it were never there. She's closed our way back.

Crap.

"What do you want?" I ask her, more bravely than I feel.

She swivels her head toward me. "You are fulfilling your promise to me. I have called, you are here. Did you pass on my message?"

"I did."

"And what is her response?"

I'm at a loss. I don't know what Lyrionna is expecting. Her message was information only. She didn't ask anything from Ellie—unless I got something wrong. The siren scrutinizes my face, then sweeps her gaze down my body. If Ellie ever made me feel as if she was weighing or measuring me, Lyrionna surpasses that in one glance. It's like she's counting my every molecule.

"Well?" Her voice is as brittle as thin ice.

"She was surprised. She couldn't believe it."

It doesn't appear that's what she wanted to hear. She lifts a lip in disgust or maybe a half-snarl.

"What are you talking about?" asks Bridgette.

I cut a glance to her, annoyed that she is drawing attention to herself. Lyrionna ignores her anyway. There is a commotion somewhere past the trees. It sounds like an argument. Lyrionna raises her head toward the noise and seems to come to some sort of decision.

"Wait here until I have calmed them," she says to the guards, I guess talking about the source of the fight we can't see. "When it is quiet, take them to the cave and watch the door. No one in, no one out." Then directly to us, "You will await me." The last is just a statement.

"You can't keep me here," Bridgette says, her voice high, eyes darting as if looking for an escape.

Lyrionna makes a noise in the back of her throat. "Be quiet. You will obey."

The command falls heavy. It's aimed at both of us. I feel it push against me, and I try not to show how I struggle with it. I see Bridgette's panic simply turn to compliance. She may not be my favorite person, but it's horrific to watch.

Lyrionna gives me a sharp glance before slipping through the filigree. As she passes, she brushes against one of the fronds and it releases pastel yellow clouds into the air. Pollen, dust, or tiny leaves, I don't know. They float suspended, like pale ink drops in water, before they dissipate. The guards remain quiet, listening, but their liquid gazes pause on me. I wonder what they make of me.

Out of sight, Lyrionna's voice cuts through the air, puncturing the babble of voices. Her tone is fierce as she admonishes the speakers, telling them to lower their voices. They speak softer, still overlapping each other. I can't make out the individual words, but they sound scared.

My mind skitters. How much time has passed above? How long until Bridgette can't breathe the way Macon couldn't here? She stares vacantly ahead like a doll. Mom doesn't know where I am. I don't know where Bridgette's parents think she is, but someone might already be missing her. No one knows where we are. I don't even know exactly where in Araem we are, after Lyrionna closed the window here. I didn't even text Macon this morning, didn't even stop at Ellie's. I should have just woken her up. I should have told her about what was happening to my mark.

This is ridiculous. I can't go wait in the cave until Lyrionna decides she wants to talk to me. Every moment here, hours—days—could be passing on Earth. I elbow Bridgette, trying not to attract the attention of the guards. She looks down where my arm made contact with hers as if vaguely interested.

"Bridgette!" I whisper, and her eyes pivot to mine. "Wake up." She blinks. There's so much salt in the air, at least I don't have to worry about having enough in my eyes. I try to pull on my power, layer my voice with command. As I open my mouth again, the guards move as one toward me.

"You must be quiet," Kiyash says.

I feel his command like feathers brushing against my skin. This is not Lyrionna; this is nothing. I smile.

"Be still." My command comes out a little more forcefully than I mean it to.

They both freeze, startled looks on their faces. I take a beat to be sure that they are listening, that this is working. "Open the passageway."

Kiyash gives me a helpless look. "I cannot."

I try again, pulling again at my power, feeling it fill my senses. "Open the way."

He lifts his hand to the air, but shakes his head. He seems pained. "I am not able."

He's not resisting me, he actually can't do as I ask. I turn to Kerin. "Open the passageway."

He struggles to obey but admits that he can't do it either. Now I'll have to find another window—hopefully one that I know. First, I have to get rid of these guys.

I speak to both of them. "You will not stop us. You will not look for us. Go to the cave and guard it as you were told."

They step back, almost in sync. Their combined gaze

slides past our faces, as they turn and walk away. I sigh in relief that they obeyed me.

Now Bridgette.

This is more delicate. I can't have her freak out, can't have her run screaming. I need to release her from Lyrionna's command, but I can't risk just replacing it with my own. I can't have her go silly the way Miss Wren did. I think about how to phrase my words. "Bridgette, come back to yourself. You don't have to obey. You don't have to wait for her." As the gentle command passes my lips, I imagine I can see it release into the dense air like the frond dust from the trees.

Bridgette blinks again, her vacant expression taking shape, resettling into the normal pissy way she looks at me.

"*Mon Dieu.* Where the hell are we?"

Chapter 30

I'm so relieved to see her normal disdain, I don't even care about her tone. I tell her quickly that we've gone through to the siren world, to Araem.

"Are-em? Are you insane?" Her eyes move from my eyes to my hair to my skin. She'll be seeing the changes this world has on me.

"There's no time for explanations." Besides what can I say, really? It's too crazy, so much to take in. To her credit, she keeps it together. Her eyes bulge a little more than usual, but surely that's to be expected.

"We're going to be okay; we're going to go back home. We just need to find a window—a way back. It has to be one I'm familiar with or we could get lost."

She looks around. "What happened to whatever we came through?"

"She closed it."

I wonder if I could remember the words she said to close it, the bit of song, maybe I could open it up again. I raise my hand and swish it around a little and try to recreate the song.

"What are you doing?" Bridgette hisses. "We should get out of here before anyone comes back."

I shrug. I hate that I agree with her. "It was worth a try," I mumble.

We edge through the trees, going the opposite direction that Lyrionna went. I tell Bridgette to be careful not to touch the branches. It would be a colored smoke signal showing that someone was walking around in here.

When we get to the tree line, I hang back. I don't see anyone in the immediate area, but I also can't quite get my bearings. The ground is multi-colored with strange vegetation just as before, but there is no clear direction. We can't just wander around. In this air with my pearly skin and swirling eyes, I might be able to pass in this world. Well, if I weren't wearing regular clothes. But with Bridgette's matte skin and normal-colored hair, she definitely can't. Only in this world would Bridgette be considered too plain. One look and anyone we meet will know we don't belong here. And running into another mini-mob is not on my to-do list.

Think, think, think! Too late I realize that maybe I should have kept the guards with us. We could have used them for cover—no one would question us if we were under guard. I could have commanded them to escort us to another passage-way. At the very least, I could have demanded that they tell me where the nearest window was and where it dumped out into our world.

"Cam, what are we doing? What's your plan?" Bridgette's voice carries an edge.

"I'm— Look, I'm working it out. I need to figure out where we are."

"Let's just go. You can just—" She flaps her hands around. "I don't know, 'woo-woo' anyone we run into."

I almost laugh at that, but before I can reply, another

boom hits, shaking the ground. I fall to my knees. Bridgette grabs a tree for support and the filigree frond tears, spilling lavender dust—spores—into the air. There is a lone scream in the in the distance and the babble of frantic discussion, altogether too close for comfort. I motion Bridgette back, deeper into the grove.

"What was—" she whispers.

I press my finger to my lips so that she'll stay quiet. She nods and her hair ripples out around her in the dense Araem air. I notice then that she doesn't appear to be having difficulty breathing—nothing like Macon did –at least not yet.

Once the voices fade, Bridgette whispers, "What happened? An earthquake?"

"Something like that. I think it's better if we don't stick around to find out."

Maybe it isn't too late to use the guards after all. At least I know which direction they went. If I can catch up to them, I could force them to help us. I motion Bridgette to follow me, changing our direction to where the guards went. She stays close on my heels, never letting too much distance separate us. I guess it's a "devil you know" kind of thing for her. I get it. I feel the same way. I know what to expect from her.

When we reach the tree line on the other side, I can see what might be the cave a little way in the distance. If it is, we're looking at it from a different angle, I think from behind it and from the opposite direction we came to it last time. Between us and it, though, are buildings that look like dwellings.

They are all in tones of the reddish-brown ground. The colors remind me of a more vibrant adobe, like we had in New Mexico. But they look nothing like the flat-roofed angular houses there. These are shaped kind of like large crescent moons facing each other, and offset so that the tip of one crescent dips into the upper hollow of another, as if they are linked together. The line of houses snakes away from where we are and then turns back on itself so that it makes a large, upside down "U" shape. It's a neighborhood. I see more of these neighborhoods farther away, but I can't exactly gauge how many houses there are.

Anyway, my focus is on the one in front of us. The bell of the "U" is closest to the cave and the open area is filled with sirens. Their metallic hair glints in the weird light. Their skin, in various shades, looks dusted in moonlight—all with that pearly sheen. A few are swathed completely in iridescent cloth as if the hoods will hide them from whatever horror is brewing.

"Too many," Bridgette says, as if picking the thought from my head.

Even if we walked along the outside of the houses, we'd have to pass by many uncovered windows. Not everyone can be in the courtyard. I study the houses and have an idea.

"Wait here," I say to Bridgette.

She shakes her head, and shifts as if she'll follow me no matter what I say. I give her a warning look, raising my hand to still her. She looks as if she wants to argue, but then gives the tiniest of nods.

The door of the house nearest us hangs open. Most of the others are shut tight. I'm hoping this means that the occupants aren't inside. Though it could mean that they'll be right back. This house curves toward the right. I can see the door in the middle of the fattest part of the crescent. Once I get near, I'll be hidden from the courtyard in the shelter of the crescent curve.

I just need to walk through the open area between the grove and house first.

The sirens in the courtyard are talking together in whispers with lots of hand gestures. They seem preoccupied. Thankfully, I don't see Lyrionna among them. I take a breath and walk out of the trees with determination, not too fast, but as if I know where I am going. I remember hearing this advice given to girls walking at night—walk with purpose, no hesitating. My heart beats unevenly in my chest, but I fake it until I reach the edge of the house and then crouch, skirting along the side to peek in the first window.

I marvel a moment at the stone that makes the house. It looks shaped, or as if it happened to grow like this, the way the inside of the cave looks. The place appears deserted, the contents ransacked as if someone was in a hurry to leave. Things forgotten or upturned on the floor. In the mess, I spy something that I think will work for what we need. I make my way to the door, listening for a few seconds until I'm sure no one is inside.

A few minutes later, I have a light, sheet-like cloth draped over my shoulders hiding my clothes as I hurry back to the grove. I give Bridgette the other cloth I took, wrapping it over her clothes and into a hood that covers her head and shades her eyes. I make a hood for myself as well. At least this way, we won't draw so much attention.

"Stay close to me," I tell her as I link my arm in hers. She stiffens at first but relaxes a little, matching her pace with mine. Just before we leave the trees, I take another deep breath. Here we go.

We walk together, as if we belong. I steer us around the outside of the neighborhood, angling for the cave. I'm pretty sure it's the right one. It rises up about the right height and has little windows ringing the top like I remember. Because there is only one entrance, we'll have to walk around to the front. A group of sirens cross our path, far enough away that they can't look too closely at us, but close enough that I hear their fierce whispers in snatches.

"…the first in an age…"

"Being silent will do nothing for us now…"

"It's her fault—she let her daughter…"

"Mind your words…" The siren who said that glances in our direction.

I keep my face impassive and head down until they pass from our hearing.

"Where's the… window?" Bridgette speaks out of the edge of her mouth.

It comes to me that I haven't bothered letting her in on my plan. She has come with me, and she has no idea where we're going. It's almost as if she believes in me.

"We're going to the guards first," I say.

She stops, but I pull her forward, forcing her to walk.

"They can tell us where to go—or take us there."

"*Sacrement*!" She says the word like a curse. "You are completely insane. We just got away from them."

"And we will again, but they know more than me."

She hesitates.

"Do you trust me?" I ask.

"Not in the slightest." At least she's honest.

"Yeah, well, do you have a choice? Now chill, or pretend to at least."

Her arm tightens on mine—her muscles going rigid with fright or anger. I try to ignore it. As we arc around to the front of the cave, we find a crowd of sirens clustered in little groups in a semi-circle around the entrance of the cave. I pull my hood a little farther forward and search past the crowd. There was a window not far from the mouth of the cave, I just don't know where it leads. If I can get the guards to give me an idea, it would be easy enough to slip through there and hope that months haven't passed in our absence. I don't let myself think about how worried Mom must be, or Macon. Just got to focus on the next—

A *boom* hits. Someone cries out. We manage to stay on our feet this time, but Bridgette's hood falls back. She snatches it forward immediately, and I glance around to see if anyone has noticed. The clusters break apart and reform in different configurations, but most are focused on the cave instead of us. The guards stand at the door, one on each side. They each have their wooden staffs out and planted in the ground between them, as if at the ready to block the door.

"Bring them out!" one siren with gold hair and reddish skin calls out. A few others raise their voices in agreement.

"They will destroy us!" shouts another.

"The Underneath wants them—let them have them!"

It takes me a second before I realize that they mean us. Somehow, those gathered here think we're in the cave and that we are chips to bargain away with The Underneath. I pull Bridgette closer to me. I think she gets it, because she holds tighter to me too. We'll never get near enough to speak to the guards with this group here.

Another *boom* hits, staggering everyone in sight. There is a noise like tearing cloth, and then it cuts off. The crowd surges toward the cave door. The guards cross their staffs, barring the entrance. I'm scanning the area for the window. It was here somewhere, and we may be better off taking chances with that than waiting to be torn apart by the crowd. The ground rumbles, and I push Bridgette in the direction I remember the window being. I can't see the distinctive shimmer. We need to get closer. There is shouting at the cave entrance and jostling all around us. Bridgette and I cling together.

Suddenly I am grabbed from behind. I jerk my free elbow

back, hoping to hurt my attacker. I think I'm aiming for a nose or solar plexus, like in a movie. I hear an intake of breath and then a familiar voice snaps at me. "Cam, come with me. Quickly."

Odele's dusky face fills my vision as she pulls Bridgette and me away from the crowd. I sag with relief, but she's urging me on. I drag Bridgette in my wake.

Chapter 31

Odele slips through the crowd like a minnow. We follow closely behind her leaving the cave and shouting sirens behind. She takes us past another copse of tree-like plants, these different from the filigree ones, a little hardier. They have thick leaves that stick straight up and remind me of kelp. Bridgette maintains pace, her breathing faster but even. She probably runs in her spare time.

The ground slopes downward and as we lose sight of the cave, Odele slows our pace and leads us into another kelp-like cluster of trees. The leaves rustle as we push through. They are smooth and slippery brushing against my hands and face, as I move past them. At least they don't release spores into the air.

"Odele, thank you. We didn't know where to go."

"You were very foolish to be out like that. Everyone is so frightened now." She sounds scared, too.

"We need to get back—back to our world, I mean." I try to remember what she called it the first time I met her. "To the Other-side. Can you show us a window—a passageway? I know there's one near the cave but—"

"It is closed. Lyrionna closed most of the ways. She thought it necessary to protect against them."

"Protect against who—or what—exactly?" Bridgette crosses her arms looking between us. She has regained some of her haughtiness, although her hands tremble.

Odele seems to really take notice Bridgette at this point. She looks her up and down, seeming curious but not very impressed. "I heard about you being here." She cocks her head. "You are so… dull." She says it in wonder and not as an insult.

Bridgette scoffs, and I stifle a laugh at the expression on her face. She slams me with a look.

"Sorry—I don't think she's trying to be mean. I think it's a translation thing."

"Whatever."

"It is simply true," says Odele.

She thrusts her arm forward, lining it up against Bridgette's. The siren's skin shines with the radiant luster of a dark pearl. Bridgette's is plainer—normal—human. I am somewhere in between. I'm getting off track. "Odele—"

"You may call me Del, if you wish." She smiles shyly, as if she's giving me a gift.

"Okay, uh, Del? Can you help us? We have to hide from the others—especially Lyrionna. Can you take us to a window that she hasn't closed? One that comes out near land?"

I'm hoping that it'll be near where we actually live, but at this point, I'd take anything that didn't put us out miles from shore or a mile underwater, for that matter. Ellie is insistent that I can't drown, but I'd rather not test it, especially with Bridgette with me.

Del hesitates. Of course. She'll want something in return. I had just rolled out of bed and am wearing no jewelry, but Bridgette…

"Give her an earring." It's not a command, just a suggestion.

"Why?" Bridgette touches her fingertips to the little sparkly studs in her ears. "They were a birthday present."

Del looks conflicted. It can't be about Bridgette's comment. I'm sure she wouldn't care. Something crosses her face, but it's gone before I can identify the expression.

"It's a thing here," I say to Bridgette. "And I don't have anything on me. We can get you new ones." I hope they are crystals and not diamonds. "Do you want to go home or not?"

"Fine." She takes out one earring and gives it to me, muttering something in French under her breath that I don't catch.

I hold out my palm to Del. "We can offer you this if you show us a window, a passageway, and tell us where it goes. It has to be near land, okay?"

Del still seems unsure, but now her eyes have latched onto the earring.

"Do you want it?" I can see that she does.

"I will take you to a window," she says, and snatches the earring in a swift movement.

DEL TELLS us to wait for her while she scouts ahead. It makes sense, and I'm grateful for her caution. She's already secured Bridgette's earring into a looping braid by her temple. I catch her gazing at the other earring, and am surprised that she doesn't try to bargain for that one as well. She disappears into the wafting leaves.

"I'm never getting that back, am I?"

"Unlikely." I don't know what else to say. But with a sinking feeling, I realize that there is something I haven't told her about being here. And I probably should before we go back. "Um, Bridgette? I need to let you know something. Time is different here."

"What is that supposed to mean?"

"You know when Macon and I disappeared?"

She flinches but nods once.

"We were here."

"That whole time? I thought you were hiding in a seedy motel or some stupid thing."

I blush; I can't help it. "No, definitely not. We were here."

Her face goes blotchy. "I can't believe you brought him here. Didn't you think it would be dangerous?"

"It wasn't my choice. Look I need to tell you…"

"I don't have to know every little thing about you two, Cam."

"You don't understand. We were here—only for an hour —maybe two."

She finally gets what I'm saying. I watch the realization hit and then settle over her. She checks her watch. Then her face drains of color, and she shakes her head in tiny movements as if she can't accept what I am saying. "How long have we been gone?"

"We won't know until we get back."

Her face says it all.

"The first time I came here, though, I was gone for ten minutes, but it only seemed to be seconds on the surface."

"How many times have you been here?"

"This is the third. Are you okay?"

She frowns at me. "I'm as good as can be expected in a place like this."

"But you aren't having trouble breathing?"

"The air is ridiculous, if that's what you mean." She takes a deep breath. "It's *comme les Caraïbes* in the summer times ten." She must notice my confusion because she clarifies with disdain. "The Caribbean. I'm fine."

"Good." Not that I'd know what the Caribbean is like during summer. I'm relieved that I don't have to try to give her my breath. And I'm glad she's not suffering. I wouldn't wish that on anyone.

We wait the rest of the time in silence until Del comes back. She tells us that she knows where to go, but she doesn't look happy about it. I ask if she's sure that the window will take us to land and she nods. I want to hug her. At least we have her on our side.

An intense *boom* hits, this one stronger than before as if it were closer to where we are. The ground shakes, and Bridgette and I grab at each other to keep upright. When it fades, she snatches her hand back. Del is crouched and shaking.

"Maybe we should try another way?"

"No!" Del shouts. "We have to go on this way. We must. It will be fine."

She doesn't look as if she wants to go on. I offer her my hand, and she takes it. Her eyes look so sad, but she motions that we should keep going. She's brave, but living with this can't be easy.

"Del, have the earthquakes been going on since I was here last?"

She gives a sad smile. "That is not what is happening. They are attacking the ways that link us to them."

"Who are 'they'?" Bridgette asks again. We never did answer her.

"This has never happened before," says Del. "There are stories and, of course, the place we go now." She shivers.

"What place? And who is trying to attack you?" Bridgette asks.

"The Underneath," says Del in a somber voice.

"Ellie explained it as another world," I say.

Bridgette rubs a hand across her forehead as if she's trying to get rid of a headache. I feel for her. It's a lot to take in. I'm surprised I'm handling it so well. Kind of well.

The kelp-like grove dumps us into a ravine. Del helps us adjust our makeshift cloaks again to cover our faces, although no one is around. We follow the ravine to the left for several minutes until the ground rises to meet an outcropping of rocks. They are the same shades of reddish-brown as the cave and the houses we saw, but these look natural. They are rough and imperfect—nothing like the smooth, sloping lines of the buildings. The rocks tower up just above my height, building on that as they move away from us and rising as high as a three-story house father away. From here, it's like the tail end of a stunted mountain range.

"Are we almost there?" Bridgette asks.

I'm sure she's worrying about the length of time we've been gone. It's playing on my mind as well. If we swing the time-moves-faster-on-Earth way, then Dad is going to freak, again. He'll use it against Mom, and I won't be there to stop it. I clench my jaw.

"Just over this rise," says Del. She casts me a worried look.

This must be taking a toll on her too. I try to think of something that could take her mind off of it as we start the climb.

"What do your builders use to get the rock so smooth?"

She slows, turning back to me. She looks like she doesn't understand the question. I pick up a loose rock from the ground. Its sharp edges press into my palm. I brush my hand over it as if I were sanding it.

"What do you use to even out the edges to shape it? What kind of tools?"

"It is not a tool. We use song."

She takes the rock from me and hums softly, while rubbing her hand across the rock. It's as though she's working with clay instead of rock. It responds to her touch, and I guess to her song. I can see the change. Then a large chunk falls away, ruining the soft line she had started.

"The Gaium do this better. They understand the stone better than I can. I do not like to wait. I always try too hard, and it breaks." She drops the rock, it lands on a clump of yellow moss-like growth, the sound muffled by the soft landing. "We should go on."

"The Guy-um? What does that mean?"

"The ones that work with rock and matter such as that." She says it as though it should be obvious, but I'm no clearer.

Bridgette picks up the rock Del dropped, running her thumb across the surface. "I can't believe this."

"I know."

She looks like she can't believe me, as if I am some sort distasteful puzzle. "But you can sing their songs." She swallows. "You can make people do what you want."

"I'm still figuring all of this out. I didn't know anything before I came here—to Shell Island, I mean. I can't sing the way Ellie can, not really."

"I saw what you did with the guards. Even after— When she made me listen. I knew what was happening around me. I just didn't care. It didn't seem as important as what she asked me to do."

"Because it feels like your own idea. The compulsion is strong." I half-laugh at her disbelieving expression. "I'm not safe from it. I have to fight against it."

Del is still trudging forward, her head dipped. We follow after her. No one is around this area. In fact, I haven't seen anyone since we first went into the kelp-like grove. I haven't heard anyone, either. If we aren't talking, our footsteps and breaths are the only sounds.

Bridgette stops, placing a hand on my arm to hold me back. "Just tell me one thing—one thing honestly. Can you do that?"

"All right, what?"

"This is what you did. You used this power on Macon, didn't you?" It's hard for her to ask me this; I can tell.

"I didn't— It doesn't work on him."

"How do you know?"

I sigh and scratch the back of my neck. I don't want to admit it. "Because I tried it. I'm not proud of it. At the time I thought it was what was best for him, but… he's immune."

She must see the truth of it in my face. She nods, but frowns as if I have confirmed something even worse. In that moment, I feel a little bad for her. If the roles were reversed, I might prefer to believe it was some unknown magic that took Macon away from me, not that his feelings had changed.

"We are here," says Del.

We've reached the top of the rise. In the shallow valley in front of us I catch a shimmer in the air that looks like a window. I rush down the hill, eager to check it, and get us home. Bridgette is close behind. As I reach the shimmer, I notice that it stretches from the ground to high above my head and is far wider than any window I've seen. A slight hum emanates from it.

I touch it and my hand meets something solid. It isn't a window, it's a barrier. I move backward several steps. The barrier stretches away on each side and upward from me. It's a bubble enclosing a football field's worth of grey, dry-looking ground. Nothing grows; it's completely desolate, a desert inside a dome. It's a giant snow globe in reverse. This is the contained area that Ellie told me about—the site of the last breach.

"You have done well, Odele," says Lyrionna, as she grasps my shoulder.

Chapter 32

My first instinct is to try to break out of Lyrionna's grip. My heart is in my throat and pulse thrumming. She's too strong. Her slender fingers dig into my shoulder. I struggle for a moment, and as I realize it's futile, I force myself to at least act calmly. As I will myself to stay still, she releases me. I elbow in front of Bridgette, putting myself between her and Lyrionna. Bridgette grabs ahold of my arm, like a reflex. Or maybe she's thinking of throwing me at Lyrionna. Odele has the decency to look ashamed, but I don't care.

I am livid. The fact that Lyrionna scares me only makes it worse. I am angry at myself. This is what I get for trusting Odele—"call me Del, if you like"—believing that she would help us. She wouldn't go against her queen, or whatever Lyrionna is to these people. Maybe she's the strongest, or maybe just the cruelest. They all seem to obey her, willingly or not.

Lyrionna's carved features are especially alien in the subtle glow of the shimmer. Her eyes swim with a myriad of changing colors. I feel if I focus on them too long, I'll get lost. Still, I fight to keep her eyes on me and to leave Bridgette alone. It isn't fair to her that she got caught up in this.

Then the ground lurches and my ears fill with a roar. The reverberation rattles me. This is what being closer to the boom feels like. There's a tearing sound again, as if someone is ripping a sheet. The shaking stops, but Lyrionna bares her teeth in a snarl.

"It may not hold!" she shouts to Odele. "Find the Aerers!"

Odele runs off to fetch whoever—whatever—Lyrionna means.

"I will not abide your defiance." This is directed at me. "You made a promise to me. I saved his life; you were to come when I summoned you."

"I did, but she wasn't part of the bargain."

"Better they left her to the elements during an attack? You are as careful with your friends as you are with your oaths."

I want to laugh at Bridgette being called my friend, but my anger is still high, made worse by Lyrionna accusing me of going back on my word. "I'm here, aren't I? Did you expect me stay?"

"I told you to await me."

"I don't have to obey you!"

"Be still!" She roars it, eyes blazing.

The command is like stepping into a hurricane—the force is so strong. I freeze, but then somehow, I resist. It starts in my belly, where my anger seems to live, banked and ready to flare at any moment. It blazes through my body, electrifying my bones and heating my muscles. It burns through me until I am able to shake off her words with one of my own.

"No." My layered voice cuts through her command, freeing me.

Lyrionna stares at me, lips parted. Then she smiles, showing her teeth. That quiet smile is more terrifying than her shouting. Her eyes seem to sharpen with interest. "So strong with you. I was right to bring you; I must know more."

She's interrupted as Del—*nope*, Odele—comes back with a few other sirens. When Lyrionna looks away, I let out a breath I hadn't realized I was holding. I turn my attention to the others. I think I recognize one of them as Kerin, the guard who came for me. The rest I've never seen.

In the aftermath of my argument with Lyrionna, I feel like I have been running for days. My legs are rubbery and my skin is hot. Bridgette comes to stand next to me, linking her arm with mine and leaning against me as if to prop me up. I must look as spent as I feel.

"That was incredible," she says staring forward.

Lyrionna and the other sirens, including Odele, are making ready to do something. They spread out with Lyrionna at the head. She starts a song and the others pick it up—overlapping each other, harmonizing. Together it lifts as though the sound has weight. They weave it like a cloth. It's mesmerizing to hear and fascinating to watch. I can make out the individual strands; the sound has physical substance. The song stretches and the strands reach for the shimmer wall, spreading out over it. They are strengthening the barrier.

The ground buckles below me as another ear-deafening *boom* shudders through my body. Bridgette and I both fall. I can't get back to my feet, because the ground is still moving. The tangible song the sirens have made changes as their singing falters. Lyrionna manages to stay on her feet and continue the song. Odele sings from her knees. Some of the strands they made snap away from the shimmer wall, like overstretched rubber bands.

Bridgette and I get up, holding on to each other. I hear the sound of cloth ripping and look for the source. It seems to be coming from all around, but I see that inside of the dome, nearly halfway into the wasteland, an uneven tear about two feet across and four feet high has appeared in the air. The edges flap in unseen wind. The opening is directly in line with where the sirens are working. Another *boom* hits, and the ground shakes. Bridgette gasps, but we stay on our feet. One of the sirens calls out. The blasts seem to affect not only the singers but their song as well, unraveling it. More strands snap, and the barrier stretches thin.

"What's happening?" Bridgette shouts.

I don't have time to answer her before the ground shakes again. A rip appears in the barrier but behind us, I hear another tearing sound. There's a passage opening from Araem into the ocean. It doesn't look right, though. Instead of being a clear-cut shimmer in the air, it looks more like the tear inside the wasteland with ragged edges. Water drips through. I've never seen that before; the windows have always appeared with clear definition between one world and the next, neither bleeding through.

Another *boom* sounds, and I watch with horror as the barrier splits open wide. A blast of hot air from the wasteland hits me. It's like opening the oven door, or walking into the summer heat of the desert. I fling an arm across my face as dust billows through the tear. It's as fine as flour and coats my hair and clothes in seconds. I look around for Bridgette. She's pulled her hood down to shield her face.

"Are you okay?" I shout, backing us away from the barrier.

She grabs my hand. *Boom.* Another rip and suddenly a wall of water rushes toward us. I shout and hold on to Bridgette tighter, as we're caught up in a tide of sea water. It rushes through, picking up people and debris, some flooding through into the wasteland. The force of the water pushes us up farther, spinning us end over end, and then sucks us back toward the tear leading to the ocean. I focus on my hand on Bridgette's, afraid we'll be torn apart. She grabs at me too, nails digging into my skin. I think I see the silver of Odele's hair and green-tinged skin of Kerin. I feel something clamp down on my ankle, but then there is too much water, too strong a current to see. I squeeze my eyes together.

I'm afraid I'll pass out. The thought comes to me seemingly from outside myself, not the terrified all-I-want-to-do-is-scream part, but the cold rational part: if I lose consciousness, I might die. Bridgette definitely would, and it'd be my fault for getting her mixed up in all this. She'd probably haunt me out of spite.

I force my eyes open. The water still moves as if agitated, but I see light through the depths. I can't tell if I am upside down or right side up. I just focus on the watery light and will myself toward it. I try to swim in this way, by will alone. It's hard with Bridgette clinging to me and the weight attached to my ankle. I kick free and push on until we break through the ocean's surface.

Bridgette gasps and coughs, over and over. I turn in a circle, legs kicking, to see where we are.

"There!" Bridgette croaks.

I doubt my own eyes. But in the distance in front of us are rocks and trees and solid ground. Farther away to the right, is a slip of beach, and up the hill a stone cottage—unbelievably, we're just off the coast of Shell Island.

Chapter 33

We push for the beach, each swimming on our own. To be fair, Bridgette swims, I flail a bit, but still make progress. I'm much less graceful above the surface of the water. As we get closer, I see Ellie on the beach. She runs into the surf to meet us and drags us up onto the sand. Then she splashes back into the water. I lie on my back staring at the clear blue sky and reveling in the sun on my face. Whatever day it is, it must be about noon. I glance over to Bridgette, who is staring at me.

She looks like a drowned rat. Her usually glossy hair is a tangled mess, and she's still wearing her siren cloak. A nervous chuckle escapes my mouth. Bridgette fights a smile but then gives way to laughing as well.

Sometimes it's all you can do.

"You look ridiculous," I tell her.

"Speak for yourself."

I look down. I'm still wearing my own jerry-rigged disguise. My bones ache, but my mind is fizzing with relief to be back on the island. Once the world stops spinning, I sit up. My clothes are covered in sand, and when I brush my hair back from my face, I end up getting it on my cheek.

Ellie is pulling someone else in from the sea. I stumble to my feet, find my equilibrium, and go to help her. It's Kerin. She waves me off, deposits him on the sand and goes back in. I follow after her to help, my strength coming back in drabs.

We pull out a total of five sirens: Kerin, Odele, two other females, and another male. The only one missing is…

Then she's there, rising mythically out of the ocean: Lyrionna. She strides through the water as if she has no patience with being tired, no room for weakness.

I twist around to find Ellie. She is frozen in mid-step, eyes fastened on Lyrionna. Her hand rises to cover a spot above her heart. Then she moves forward three steps before halting again. Her expression reflects disbelief, and for the first time, I see plain uncertainty on her face.

Ellie waits and lets Lyrionna close the gap between them. I make my way toward them. I don't know what I think I can do in this situation, but something in the way Ellie holds herself makes me realize that I can't leave her to face Lyrionna alone.

"They broke through," Lyrionna says. "They ripped their way into Araem and pierced the barrier sealing the wasteland. They tore a hole into this world, too. I think I was able to patch the barrier, and to close the tear to this world, but I could not reach the tear inside the wasteland. I do not know if the barrier will hold for long. I do not know what will happen —" She looks around in dismay. "Is this all who made it to the surface?"

Ellie says, "I do not know… mother." The word is colored with so many feelings, I wonder if Ellie even knows which one to pick.

ELLIE AND LYRIONNA help the others to the cottage. Bridgette and I help Kerin, though he'd been our guard just a little while ago. Everyone looks shell-shocked but amazed by the cottage, the furnishings, and the stove. Ellie tells me to get down mugs for stew.

"Wait— I have to know. How long were we gone?"

She frowns at me, puzzled.

"What day is it?"

"It is Sunday."

"Which Sunday?"

She tells me the date and I realize that it's the same day we left. While I digest that, she continues. "Your mother has not yet come to me. I saw that boat by the water, but could not see you. I heard the sounds from the water and found you there. You were not supposed to go back in."

I put the mugs next to the stove, and Ellie starts to fill them. I still can't get past the time. "They came for me at dawn. Bridgette got taken as well. We were gone for nearly a whole day. How is it still Sunday?"

"I told you before, you cannot predict it. Pass these out."

She presses two mugs into my hands, and I give them away and come back for more. Lyrionna sits regally in the chair in the living room. The cottage feels bursting with so many people in it.

Ellie even gives Bridgette a mug. She sips it, takes a small swallow, then grimaces and sets it down. I wonder vaguely how it tastes to her human tongue. Ellie tells me where to find extra towels, and we pass them out. Kerin holds his up as if unsure what he's been given. One of the women rubs the cotton between her fingers and then against her face. Ellie watches the other sirens longingly, as if she can't believe they are there, like they represent something she has lost.

Once everyone is as settled as they can be, Ellie asks what

happened. Lyrionna doesn't mention snatching us off the dock, but tells about the attacks. They had started when Macon and I were there, but after we left, things calmed. The scouts were still visible, so the tide hadn't turned, but they were testing the boundaries less and less.

Then something changed. There was a renewed effort— the attacks were harsher, more earnest, and coming more frequently.

"What caused this?" asks Ellie.

"I am not certain, but I am beginning to believe it is connected to this one." She points at me.

"Camline? Why would you think that?"

"You named her Camline?" Lyrionna's eyes wash over me.

"I did not name her, her parents did, but I told my daughter of the name."

I wonder what's so interesting about my name, but Lyrionna is talking again.

"I called her back, and she tried to depart without my leave." This is a pure accusation. "I did not call the other one."

Ellie lifts an eyebrow at Bridgette. "Curious about the lives of others, Bridgette Dupuis? I remember your grandmother."

Bridgette's eyes flash momentarily, but then she relents. "I was trying to help Cam. They were kidnapping her." She sounds exasperated.

"Misguided bravery, then."

Ellie says nothing about the fact that clearly Bridgette knows about sirens now. I skip past that myself because something Lyrionna said before is just now registering. "Hang on a second, how could I be responsible for more attacks? I wasn't even in the water."

Lyrionna narrows her eyes but doesn't respond. Ellie looks thoughtful.

"When did the increase come?" I ask.

"Yesterday."

Saturday. I was nowhere near the water then. I didn't even go to the coast. I was in the clearing with Macon. Assuming the time even vaguely matches up.

"Did you see them? Did they break all the way through?" Ellie asks.

"Some of the Aerers and I tried to fortify the barrier, but they were able to rip it, and it tore into this world as well. As I said, I sealed that but could not close the tear inside the wasteland. I wove the barrier back together—made something that might work temporarily but we— I need help."

That last seems to cost her to admit.

Chapter 34

"Camline, take your... friend to Windemere. Tell your mother to join me when she is able." Ellie says.

I want to argue. I don't think I should leave her here on her own with the others, but Ellie's expression stops the words from coming out of my mouth. She wants me out of the cottage. Besides, I have the feeling that what she really meant was for me to tell Mom to come immediately.

"Come on," I say to Bridgette. "You can borrow some clothes." She lifts her eyebrows at that but follows me.

Mom meets us at the door of Windemere. She is wearing a robe over sweatpants and a T-shirt and carrying a coffee mug. When she catches sight of us, she seems to realize that this is not our usual lazy Sunday.

I try to calm her while she scolds me for leaving my phone and peppers me with questions about where I was this morning, why we're wet, what the heck I'm wearing, and who the girl next to me is.

"I know her from school. She was visiting..."

"I'm Bridgette Dupuis."

"Oh you are, are you?" Mom's tone is soft, but she grips her mug tighter.

I haven't told her much about Bridgette, but maybe she remembers Anne's comment. Oh God. I need to text Macon.

"Hang on, that's not important. Ellie sent me away because her house is filled with sirens. She needs you."

"What?" Mom's jaw drops.

I give her the briefest outline of what happened. She seems really angry that I kept the changes to the mark secret, saying that we'd talk about that later. She gives Bridgette an appraising look when she must realize that she knows about me—about all of us. Mostly she listens, asking pertinent questions, whole body on alert.

"Lyrionna is *here*?" She exclaims when I get to the end.

"Yeah, with some others. Ellie gave them stew."

Mom laughs without humor at that. She gathers some blankets, and as she rushes out the door, tells me to "stay put." Yeah right.

Bridgette is shorter than me and has more shape in her petite figure, so my jeans would probably be a bit too tight and way too long. I give her a pair of leggings and a long-sleeved T-shirt and point her to the bathroom. I tell her she can shower if she wants, but she shakes her head. She's been pretty quiet since I told Mom the story. I guess it's hard to believe any of that happened when we're standing inside the solidness of Windemere. She doesn't share her thoughts with me, and I don't ask.

I check my phone and then change as fast as I can. Macon has sent five texts. The first and second are just a "hello" and "checking that you got my text" but the urgency increases rapidly in the texts after those. I call him, but it goes to voicemail.

I text back: **I'm here. I'm OK. Have news—big news. Call me.**

My phone buzzes. It's an email from Dad that I ignore. But there's also something from Jane. I click on it. She found the adoption company, but they are no longer in business, which is probably why we didn't find anything on our first search. She has attached two documents: one with "birth certificate" in the title and the other is a letter.

Before I can click on either, Bridgette knocks on the door and then walks in. The leggings are too long on her, bagging a little at the ankles, but she fills out my T-shirt better than I do.

"Do you have a bag?" She holds her sandy, soaking clothes.

I hurry to get her one from the kitchen. No matter what Mom said, I have to get back to the cottage.

"I'll make sure you get back to your boat."

She opens her mouth to reply but is cut off by a knock at the door.

"Yeah?"

Macon bursts in. "You're okay! I thought you disappeared again. Why didn't you—"

He stops short as he sees Bridgette next to me. He looks from her to me and back, presumably noticing how she's dressed. "Tell me everything."

"She got caught in my mess."

"What the hell?"

Bridgette pipes up, "I know, but get past it. I think there's a war coming."

He looks to me for explanation.

"The Underneath broke through and now there's something happening in Araem. Well, potentially. Lyrionna said that she may have stopped it. I don't understand fully. Bridgette, you should go. Your parents must think—"

"They know where I am. They just don't know I am with you, Cam."

That lands awkwardly. Of course, her parents would assume that she was visiting Macon if she came out to the island. I don't look at either of them, super conscious of their shared history.

Macon clears his throat. "Cam's right, you should go home."

"I'm not going anywhere." She lifts her chin, face set. "I don't think I'd be any safer in the boat. And besides, you might need my help."

I study her face. She has raked her hair into a haphazard bun. Sand grains thread through it. There's a bruise coming up on her cheek.

"Okay," I say.

"What? Since when do you two agree?"

I shrug. "A lot's happened."

I fill him in as quickly as possible, wondering how many times I'm going to have to tell the story.

"I need to get back to the cottage, find out what's been decided. And make sure no one is killing anyone."

"I'm coming too," he says.

"You realize that Lyrionna is one of the sirens who came back with us?"

"Exactly. You aren't going there by yourself."

"But— I think she may be worse for you." She had been so *interested* in Macon. The way she watched him gasp for breath.

"It's not your decision, Cam. You go, I go."

Bridgette purses her lips and rolls her eyes.

≈

WHEN WE WALK OUTSIDE, I remember Jane's email.

"I meant to tell you... I asked Jane to do a little research for us. About what we were talking about yesterday. I'll send it to you."

"Right. Thanks."

"Did your mom say anything more?"

He glances at Bridgette. "Nope. Maybe Jane had better luck?"

"There are a couple of attachments— I haven't seen them yet."

I forward the email while we're walking. As we get closer to the cottage, we hear raised voices. "Last chance..." I say to both—either—of them. Neither backs down.

Bridgette drops her bag outside, and the three of us walk into the cottage together. Mom doesn't look pleased to see me, and her scowl deepens when she notes the other two with me. She's sitting on a chair pulled from the dining table. Lyrionna is still in the armchair, but she sits hunched forward over the coffee table with one of the females and Kerin. The others are scattered around like bewildered dolls. Odele is wrapped in a blanket, sitting on the floor, focused on the coffee table discussion. Ellie watches from the kitchen.

As they are drying, the sirens look less foreign, in the same way a shell taken from the beach never shines the same when you get it home. Maybe it's the salt, but I think part of it is the fact that they are away from their home. Out of context. If their skin fades to more normal hues and their hair loses its metallic shine on land, are their eyes affected too? As human as they're starting to look, they all wear strangely cut clothes made from cloth you definitely can't get in Williams Point.

"If we do not know what is happening, how can we fight?" says Kerin, gesturing to the coffee table.

"We know this whole area is compromised," says Lyrionna, picking up a mug and setting it down with force. "Even if the barrier holds, much of the air in that area is tainted."

I notice that they have arranged the mugs as if each one stands for a section. They are making a plan.

"We do not know what happened to the others. They could be trapped there, or gone through to somewhere else in the ocean," says the other female at the table.

Mom gets up and comes over to me. "Go back to the house, and you two go home."

"No," says Lyrionna. "They should stay and explain what they have done."

"We—" I start, but Mom jumps in.

"They did nothing. They're just kids. They aren't part of this."

"You, land boy, come here." There's still enough water in her eyes, that I feel the command reach for him. It's strong, but nothing close to what it was when we were in their world. Everything seems amplified there.

"My name is Macon." He stays where he is.

"Why do you not heed me?" Her voice is dangerously low.

"Leave him alone," I say.

Her eyes shoot to mine and then to Ellie's. "This one can fight me as well." At least two of the other sirens gasp. Lyrionna continues. "Her blood is strong. Even if it is diluted." She says the last with disdain.

"Yes." Ellie doesn't say any more than that simple word, but it drops heavy in the room. Odele and Mom both look startled by this news, and the others seem frightened.

Lyrionna narrows her eyes, then asks Macon, "Where do you come from?"

"Here?" He shrugs, as if to say this is obvious.

"There is something else in you. Unlike her." She nods to Bridgette.

"It doesn't matter right now," I say. "What's happening in Araem?"

"It matters the most," says a female who had been leaning against the wall. She is swathed in a blanket. Her skin is ruddy and her light red hair is shot through with glints of bronze. A shell bracelet rattles on her wrist. "They do not listen to you. We cannot trust them. She cannot be one of us. Ellianna is hardly one of us anymore."

"Have care, Araline. I am who I am. Your words or even this land I'm tied to cannot change that, *sister*." Ellie's presence fills the small room. It even crowds against Lyrionna, who regards Ellie with appraisal. Everyone goes quiet for a moment.

I'm thinking about Ellie's use of the word sister. Does she mean by blood, or is that just what she calls the others? Araline looks nothing like Ellie or Lyrionna, so I think it must be the latter.

Then Kerin speaks in his voice like gravel. "The young one is right. We need to know what damage has been done. And then we can see if anyone else is hiding there. I'm certain Kiyash lives, and he will protect those he finds. Or if they went somewhere else, perhaps we can track them." He gestures toward the woman next to him. "Hivanna and I can return to scout."

"I will go too, Kerin," says Araline.

"I do not want to send any of you until we know more," says Lyrionna, sitting back into the chair.

"What happened before?" I ask. "Why did they get through the last time?"

"None of us were alive then," says Hivanna. She holds an

oyster shell like a talisman, rubbing her thumb inside its curve.

"But you have history, right? What's written?"

Hivanna laughs, not unkindly. She has a dimple in her upper cheek. Kerin smiles, it gentles his face. Ellie answers me. "We do not write in Araem. We tell stories."

I guess I never saw a book in the siren world. "Okay then, what do the stories say?"

Araline gives an exasperated sigh. "Children's stories will not help us now."

"Children's stories?" I look to Ellie for help.

"We pass on knowledge through stories. They can change depending on the circumstances, so there may be many different versions. Storytellers adjust them to make them fit a situation."

Something like this seems important enough to keep a good record, but I don't say that. I try a different tactic. "We have our own children's stories. They talk about you." I indicate the sirens. "Or something like you. Most of it is nonsense, but I can see now that there is a kernel of truth within them."

Odele speaks up then. "One story about the last breach is that during a tide shift, two bad children, a boy and a girl, disobeyed their parents because they wanted a treat. They were told to be silent on this day, but they were greedy, selfish children. They cried so loud that a creature from The Underneath heard them. She promised them something delicious to eat if they would just sing a hole in the world. But she was tricking them. Once they sang, The Underneath broke through. It took the essence from the land and air and even ate the little girl. But the Aerers sang and closed the way to The Underneath. They sang the barrier, sealing the wasteland. And this has stood for all time."

"I was told that it was the boy who was eaten," says Kerin. "It is just a story to make the children behave. 'Stop your crying or The Underneath will get you.'"

"I heard it differently," says a quiet voice from the floor. It's the other male siren. I'd almost forgotten he was there.

"What did you hear?" Mom asks.

"That it was a prisoner escaping who persuaded someone to open a gate, or in some versions, she opened it herself. She had been taken from a different world—not ours—and only needed to pass through to go home. Something from The Underneath followed her, stealing the essence of the world in its quest. The Aerers sang the barrier. I've also heard that they were not strong enough without the help of the prisoner."

Araline speaks up then. "No, not a prisoner, she was a spy from a foreign land. She pretended to need help and persuaded the children to open a door. Then The Underneath broke through and ravaged the land. The spy was sorry and so helped the Aerers build the barrier."

Someone chimes in saying the spy didn't feel bad but was forced to help. Someone else argues that the Aerers didn't need her help. They talk over each other.

"What are 'air-ers'?" Bridgette asks me in a whisper.

I shake my head. I have no clue.

Ellie answers her. "Those who have the ability to shape substance from nothing."

I hadn't realized she had moved nearer to us.

"Can you do that?" I want to know.

"Not as good as them." She nods to the other sirens in the room. "We all can sing, but usually have a strength in one area."

I remember the chunk of rock falling off the stone when Odele was singing to it. She said others were better at it.

"The buildings— They are shaped from the rock. Made

by…" I try to remember what Odele called them. "The Gaium?" I stumble over the unfamiliar word.

"Yes. They shape stone and sand, to create the spaces around them."

My mind ticks. Ellie's house is made from stone but was built, not shaped. I've never seen her make something out of thin air. Maybe there's more.

"What's yours?"

"I am Vivoem. I sing to that which lives, or has done. I sing to wake."

It makes sense with the way she treats the hides. "What's Mom?"

"She is like me."

"What am I?"

"That remains to be seen."

Macon has been following our hushed conversation. He shifts his eyes toward the armchair. "What's Lyrionna?" he asks Ellie.

"She is everything. And more."

Chapter 35

Mom calls for quiet in the babble of siren voices arguing about the stories. "There are similar elements in each story. One: someone, a female, comes from The Underneath. Two: The Underneath destroys the land. Three: the Aerers close the way and build the barrier—possibly with her help."

Mom's right, but something is bugging me. "What happened to the prisoner? Or spy or trickster—whatever she was?"

Macon nods. "That's right. None of the stories say what happened to her."

I continue. "Yeah, whether she helped or didn't with the barrier, she just disappears."

"But what exactly is The Underneath?" Bridgette asks in a small voice.

"Enough." Lyrionna stands up. "Araline is right, we surely will not find the answers in children's stories. Kerin, you have my leave. Take Hivanna and Araline, if she wishes. Go in stealth and assess the damage. See if the patch holds. Gather anyone you find. Bring me every Aerer you can. We will strengthen the barrier again and close the tear inside it."

The three sirens she mentioned rise to their feet immediately. The other male also stands. He isn't as tall as Kerin or as powerfully built, but he still looks strong.

"I will go as well. Another pair of eyes, another voice to sing if required."

Lyrionna dips her head. "Thank you, Miron. No, Odele, you will stay with me," she says, when the young siren opens her mouth. Then to Kerin, "Do not take foolish chances. I expect you back as soon as possible."

"How will they go back? Aren't a lot of the ways closed?" I ask.

"We should go back the way we came through," says Kerin. "It puts us in the best place to see if the barrier holds."

"If you go to the passageway that I sealed, you can go through there," Lyrionna says. "I left a mark visible to our eyes. Araline, you will be able to open it and close it again."

"I'll take you down to the coast. We could go to the beach again, but you'll want to be farther east on the island to line up with where we came out." I tell them.

Mom looks as if she doesn't like this idea; I tell her that it'll be easier if we show them.

"They cannot be lost in the water," says Lyrionna.

"It could help their speed," counters Ellie.

"Macon will come with me." I look to him for confirmation.

"And me," says Bridgette.

Lyrionna seems swayed by the argument. Mom grips her cane tightly, but agrees that we take them. I wonder if she would have allowed it if she wasn't holding a reminder of her own limitations. The sirens shed their blankets and follow us out.

We make quite a ragtag band. We three with four sirens in

tow. They look around as we walk. Everything must look so different and strange to them. I was exactly the same way in their world. I watch Hivanna brush her green-tinged hands across the needles of a tree we pass and jerk back as if it pricked her. She puts her finger in her mouth and grimaces. I grin. Pine is great to smell, but I wouldn't want to eat it. She catches eyes with me and smiles back, showing her dimple. It softens her harsh exterior with her lean muscles and fighter's walk.

I ask Macon if there's a path from the beach to the mid-island area, which is where I estimate we surfaced.

"Not along the coast—at least not an easy path. We can take them as far as we can from the beach, or we could go through the woods and then make our way north from the clearing."

"We will be faster in the water," Kerin says.

We angle east and north to the far edge of the small beach and walk with them to the surf.

"How do you know it's safe to go into the water?" I wonder aloud.

"We do not know. We do as we must." Kerin mitigates his words with a half-smile.

"You guys be careful." I feel like their mom, sending them off.

Even Araline smiles at that, but she doesn't look at me. We watch them walk into the surf, waves catching at their feet and clothes. Then they dive together and disappear from sight.

WHEN WE'RE NEARLY BACK to the cottage, Macon asks Bridgette if she'll go home now. She says she doesn't want to be on the water, but I wonder if she's just afraid of missing something.

"You have to call your mom, though. Or she'll be calling mine."

I'd forgotten about Anne for a minute. "Where does your mom think you are, Macon?"

"Um, she wasn't there when I left."

"Maybe you should both go to your house."

Macon raises his eyebrows at me. Even Bridgette looks surprised.

"Anne loves you. If Macon shows up with you, maybe she won't be mad. You can call your mom from there. We don't know when Kerin and the others will come back. And I don't think you should spend more time than necessary with Lyrionna, Macon."

"Why does she look at you like that?" Bridgette asks. "And why does their... power not work on you?"

"I have no idea—about either. But I'm glad it doesn't."

Bridgette scowls as if she's trying to figure it out. She picks up her bag of soaking clothes from outside Ellie's cottage and they leave.

I watch them walk off through the trees and try not to give into the tiny hooks of jealousy trying to snag my attention.

MOM SEEMS relieved when I walk back through the door. Lyrionna is still sitting in the armchair, looking as regal and aloof as ever. Odele regards me with sad eyes when I come in. My mouth twitches, but I don't think I'm ready to forgive her. Ellie pours me a mug of stew without asking. I slurp it down like I didn't just have one a couple of hours ago.

I tell Mom that Bridgette is walking back with Macon

and, when she raises her eyebrows, assure her that it was my idea. Maybe my stupid idea, but my idea anyway. They should make good time. If they don't stop at the clearing. If they do, will he tell her about what happened to him there?

Macon had suggested that we take the sirens to the ocean through the clearing. That it would be around the area in the ocean that I described as where we surfaced. If it is, then the clearing would be in an almost direct line from the island to the tear into Araem, where the wasteland is.

I pull out my phone to check Jane's email again. I also have a text from her asking if I got the email. I text her back and thank her, letting her know that I'd also sent it on to Macon. She writes back immediately.

Pretty crazy wasn't it? What'd he say?

I have no idea what is supposed to be crazy, so I open the attachments. The letter is confirming a visit from the Child and Family Services Department. The birth certificate lists his name and birthdate. His mother is listed as "Alice L. Carroll." That name sounds familiar to me… Something from a long time ago. Father is listed as "Unknown." But Macon's birthplace is listed as Shell Island, Maine. Macon told me that he had come to the island when he was a few months old, but if the birth certificate is right…

"Ellie? Do you know about this?"

Ellie glances at me from the kitchen, but Lyrionna calls to me.

"Come to me for a moment." It isn't a command. "Please."

It's the "please" that gets me. I click my phone so the screen goes black and slip it into my pocket. Ellie follows me into the living room, and Mom sits up straighter.

"Yes?" I hang back several feet, near Mom's chair.

Lyrionna moves her eyes over my face and body as if she's inspecting a new find. I don't flinch. Well, not much.

"Different than I expected. You both are." The last is directed at Mom. "Although this land does not agree with you. Any of you."

Ellie puts one hand on my shoulder and the other on Mom's. We may fight among ourselves, but here we are united.

"You know I speak true, Ellianna. Look at your daughter."

Mom starts as if Lyrionna's words have physical impact.

"She's fine," I say. We're on dangerous ground.

"Is she?" Her voice is cold and clinical. "The land depletes her. Her strength fails. She must have a stick to walk."

Ellie stiffens next to me, but I can't hold back the fury building inside. "You have no idea what you're talking about. You don't know us—or anything about our lives. You don't belong here. I never knew you existed until you took Macon and me into the sea."

Her eyes spark. "Yes, the land boy you brought to our world. You caused this chaos."

She's unbelievable. We wouldn't have gone if she hadn't pulled him under. I had no choice.

"Stop talking to my daughter like that." Mom is on her feet, steady and strong, her tone fierce.

Lyrionna rises and the room seems to get colder. Odele watches with wide eyes, looking between us and the older siren. Lyrionna is impressive, even with her hair drying to the same blonde and white as Ellie's, even with her skin dulling in the air, even with a threadbare blanket sliding off her shoulders. She is other, she is…

"Mother, stop." Ellie's voice is pitched low but made of steel. She steps in front of Mom and me, arms outstretched as if protecting us. She is several inches shorter than Lyrionna, but you wouldn't know it by the way she's standing. She's not daunted. "Camline is correct. You do not know us."

"That is because you left. To live here on dry land."

"I had love. It was your choice to sever contact. Your choice for me to be tied here."

"And where is your love now?"

Ellie's intake of breath is a hiss. I know that has to hurt, but she doesn't back down. She takes a beat before saying, "You came to me. You are the guest here."

Something like regret or maybe even chagrin crosses Lyrionna's face. But before she can answer, my phone starts to ring. I didn't even know I had the ringer on. I fumble with it to turn it off, but I see that it's Macon. I turn away and answer the call.

His panicked voice crackles loudly over the line, filling the hush in the room. "Cam, it didn't work! Something's coming! Hurry now! The clearing—"

Then the line goes dead.

Chapter 36

I punch my thumb at the phone to reconnect twice before I realize that I am just wasting time. Mom's face is ashen, and even Ellie looks rattled. Lyrionna takes a step back, and Odele springs to her feet.

"We have to go," I say uselessly, for everyone is already in motion. "Mom, you should stay here."

"Not a chance—just go, I'll catch up."

We all push out of the cottage together. Odele starts toward the beach.

"Through the woods," I call to her.

"Lead!" shouts Lyrionna, and for once, I don't care that she's telling me what to do.

I set off in a run, Lyrionna next to me, and Ellie on my other side. Odele follows. I glance back to see where Mom is, and she's making good time, using her cane to help her.

The forest wraps around us as we enter through the trees, our stampeding footsteps sending a flock of small birds into the sky. It's still light out, but it's darker in the woods. My breath comes fast, and my heart thunders in my ears. But I don't flag, Macon's voice still ringing in my ears. He sounded terrified.

"This way!" I lead the others off the path, over a dead log, and through the brush. We burst through the trees into the clearing. Empty. I run into the center and scream Macon's name. Nothing. The usual peace and tranquility of the clearing is disturbed. My breath comes in pants. The others fan out, everyone looking around for the danger. I think I catch a glimpse of a glow, but it fades. It must have been a trick of the light. Only it was by Macon's tree...

"Macon! Bridgette!" I shout again.

From the woods at the top of the clearing, I hear something. I run on, calling their names. The others crash behind me. My focus is ahead of me as I dip and swerve around trees, leaping over stones. I hear another shout and press forward even faster. "This way!"

The trees thin and there they are, standing by the rocks on the bluff overlooking the ocean. Something lies on the ground between them. Macon rushes to meet me, and I throw myself into his arms, both of us skidding on pine needles. His clothes are wet.

"What happened? What's going on?" I'm still shouting.

"Cam!" Bridgette sounds like she's bordering on hysteria. The bottoms of her leggings are soaked.

She's kneeling over something on the ground. It takes a moment for my brain to understand what I'm seeing. It's Kerin collapsed in a heap.

Lyrionna reaches him just as I do. Ellie pushes past and orders Lyrionna to help her lay him out. She does as she's asked without a blink. Odele cries out when she sees Kerin's still figure. Mom arrives, red-faced. Bridgette looks stricken and Macon— Macon looks shocked.

"Are you okay?"

He brushes off my concern. Then he cocks his head like he's listening. "There are more out there…"

We both run to the edge and look down. Araline is climbing up, one hand holding on to the rocks, the other to Miron. Macon jumps down to a flat area to help Miron while Araline climbs the rest of the way. I give her my hand at the end.

I scan past her to the rocks and waves further out. "Where's Hivanna?"

Araline shakes her head. She sees Kerin, and stumbles toward him. Ellie looks her up and down in an instant and then dismisses her, focused on Kerin and the scorch mark in the middle of his chest. She sings to him, low and melodic. It's similar to the complicated melody I have heard before but has another layer added in. Lyrionna stands at the rocks looking out over the water, her heard turning as if searching. Kerin opens his eyes and sits up, looking dazed.

"Miss Ellie!" Bridgette calls her over to where she is kneeling by Miron.

There's a deep burn or gash on his arm. Blood flows freely down it, pooling on the ground. It's too much blood. Ellie wipes it away, inspects the cut, and tells me to fetch some sea water. Then she changes her mind.

"No, wait— Do not go in the water. You, Araline, come here."

Ellie takes hold of the end of Araline's tunic and squeezes it over Miron's cut. As she does she hums to it.

"Why didn't the sea water help when he swam through it?" I ask her.

"It did. This was much worse."

I shudder because it already looks pretty freaking bad to me.

Lyrionna turns back from the coast and sweeps her gaze over all of us here. "It did not hold?" she asks Kerin.

"There is a break, a rift in the barrier... It's getting larger." He takes a breath. "The work we did—you did—before we came to the surface helped, but when we tried to fortify it, we were attacked. Hivanna is dead." Pain clouds his face.

"What attacked you?" Lyrionna presses, as if she can't see how distressed he is.

"Scouts only. I recognized their shape. There were two. We injured one, but could not fend off the other." He seems ashamed by admitting this.

"They will call others; they will call their masters."

Kerin nods his head in assent. "But— It is strange, they did not seem to be searching for us. When Araline opened the passage and we went through, at first, they ignored us as if we didn't matter."

Lyrionna pauses while this sinks in. She flicks her eyes in my direction and frowns. I can't read her expression.

Kerin continues. "They attacked when we tried to force them back into the wasteland."

"And the others?" Lyrionna asks.

"We saw no one else. The whole area near the wasteland was empty."

I speak up then. "That was empty when we were there. After we left the—trees? The green grove?" I have no idea what they call them. I look to Bridgette for support. She nods. "When we climbed the rise next to the wasteland, we didn't see anyone else. Except Odele..." I purse my lips for a microsecond. "And you."

Even in the midst of this, I'm still annoyed that Odele fooled me. I go on. "Maybe people are still in their homes or at the cave. We saw a lot of people near there earlier."

"It is possible," says Araline. "But we were cut off.

There's no way past the rise—the rift is open and pouring dead air into Araem. There's no way to know if there are others out there."

"They could have gone through to elsewhere in the oceans," says Miron.

Ellie had said there were other portals "anywhere there is ocean." So maybe they escaped to the North Sea or something, but if Lyrionna had closed most of the windows, how would they escape? Maybe she left markers for their eyes the way she did with the one by the wasteland.

"If there are only two scouts and still some of our people left, we could bring a force," Lyrionna says.

"There were only two scouts then; we do not know how many may have come through now." Kerin's face is bleak.

"Then I will go, to try again," says Lyrionna.

"What can you do, Mother, on your own?" Ellie asks her.

"I must try."

"I could go with you. If you lift my bond."

Bond? Ellie never leaves the island. She said she could when my grandfather was alive, but after he disappeared, she was stuck on the island. She told me that it was the bargain she made. But— Her own mother did this to her? Her own mother kept her away from her home, stranded her here.

"Momma, wait." Mom takes Ellie's arm as if she's going to physically stop her from leaving.

Ellie touches her face, smiles just to her, and then turns back to Lyrionna. "You came to me for help. What help did you think I could give if I was still bound to this land? I am not an Aerer, but I know the song. Lift my mark; I will come."

Lyrionna's brow wrinkles. I don't know if it's about this mark or if she's worried. The others stand and say they will go, too. Kerin is unsteady on his feet. Miron's wound is healing, although he lost a lot of blood. I don't think that can be replenished by sea water. Araline stands tall, but looks tired. Odele is fierce, yet I still see the twelve-year-old girl in her face.

"What about me?" I might not know a lot, but I could help. I could do something. They could teach me the song. Macon looks at me, alarmed. He steps toward me, but Bridgette puts a hand on his arm. She and I share a look. She saw the wasteland. She knows what The Underneath did to Araem. That they could do the same here is unthinkable. Macon shakes off Bridgette's hand and comes to stand by me.

"What songs does she know?" Lyrionna asks Ellie.

Before she can answer, Mom says, "I still remember. I could help, too."

Ellie shifts. "I do not know. Serena, you are still recovering, and Camline, you are too—"

"I'm older than Odele." I guess at how she was going to finish that sentence.

"You came to me, Mother, I will go," Ellie says to Lyrionna.

"We need all the help we can get," says Kerin.

Macon turns to me. He clearly isn't happy about the way the conversation is going.

"I have to go. It's worth the risk," I say to him.

He shakes his head. "I don't think it is."

"We'll all be together. Ellie will be there."

"You heard what Ellie said. Your mom is still sick and you don't know anything."

That brings me up short for a second. "And *you* heard what Kerin said. They need all the help they can get."

"But what can you do? And how long will you be gone?"

I'm pretty sure this is all coming from him looking out for

me, but it still rankles. "Macon, I don't know what's going to happen, but I have to try. This is my family."

"You could help from here." He looks as if he thinks I'm being stubborn.

"Not as well."

I walk away, my heart dragging. We're not going to resolve this now, and there's no time. I hurry to catch up with the others. He and Bridgette follow us down to the rocks.

Lyrionna pulls Ellie to the side. There's still one more thing that must be done before we can leave. "This would be easier if he were here as well," she says to Ellie.

"That is a bond you cannot unravel, Mother, just lift the tie to the island."

She pulls her shirt down to expose her shoulder and the area above her heart. There is a mark similar in color to mine but a different shape, like two spirals end to end and overlapping in the middle.

Lyrionna puts a hand over the mark and says, "I did not mean for it to be forever."

Something passes over Ellie's face. I can't tell what.

Lyrionna sings, and as she does, I *see* the sound. It's just as when they were creating the barrier, the sound takes shape and lifts, little filaments slipping toward the mark. The song knows exactly where to go.

I look at Macon. In the madness of getting here and treating the wounded, I haven't even asked him. "How did you know?"

"Know what?" He isn't looking at me. His face is set as if he's angry with me.

"How did you know to come to the ocean?" I turn to Bridgette. "Why were you still in the woods?"

"We went to the clearing," says Bridgette.

"I thought I heard something, you know, like before." Macon continues.

Bridgette interjects. "You panicked. I didn't know what was going on. He called you, Cam, and then just took off through the trees. I went after him, and then we saw Kerin in the water. We went into the ocean and pulled him up to the top."

That's why their clothes are wet. "What did you hear, Macon?"

"I—" He looks around.

Kerin and Araline are having a low conversation, I think about weapons. Odele looks away when she catches my eye. The others are watching Lyrionna work with Ellie.

"What was it?" I say, just to him. I'm putting some things together, but I don't understand it fully yet...

"The tree. I heard the tree screaming. She said something was wrong in the ocean."

As I try to wrap my head around that, Ellie gasps, pulling my attention back to her. Lyrionna's song increases in complexity and volume. It looks as if the song threads are physically pulling the mark right off of Ellie's skin. She hisses. It must hurt. The mark is caught in a net of song filaments. The spirals unwind and then the mark fades away. Where the spirals had intertwined, a ghostly remnant remains.

Odele is watching me. "Did you see?" She sounds surprised.

"That was amazing. Ellie, are you okay?"

Ellie flinches and rolls her shoulder. "I am. Let us go... home." I can see her anticipation, even though we're not sure what awaits us there.

"Follow me to where the tear was, near the wasteland. Do not try to open it. I will open it when we are all there. I will need to seal it again as soon as possible." Lyrionna tells us, as we stand on the rock edge. "Do you know the way, Ellianna?"

"I cannot be lost in the water." She smiles at that. "Serena, Camline, stay close to me."

I give Bridgette a quick squeeze—as much to my surprise as hers. "Thank you."

Then I turn to Macon.

"Don't go, Cam," he says.

"Cam could see the song," Odele says, mostly to Lyrionna.

Lyrionna gives me a considering look. "You can help with the barrier."

Macon looks upset.

"You see?" I say to him. "I have to go. I have to. I'll come back. I promise."

He holds me tightly for a second, and I hope that I haven't just lied to him.

Chapter 37

Underwater, my vision clears and sharpens, like a camera coming into focus. Colors are multi-layered and extend beyond the normal spectrum. We don't even have names for all the colors I can see with salt in my eyes. Everything looks more real—sharper, cleaner. I will never get used to this.

We move through the water like we're flying. I hang on to Mom and she to Ellie. They, too, are transformed underwater. Their eyes swirl with colors, their skin is iridescent. Ellie's hair is the same as Lyrionna's: gold shot with silver. Mom's is mostly her normal honey-brown but with metallic highlights. They are agile in the water, as am I. I could spend an hour just looking at them. But as fast, as graceful, as we may be, we lag behind the others. Their metallic flashes are far ahead.

When they stop, I know we are close. We gather where the window was. Lyrionna presses a finger to her lips, as if any of us needs reminding that stealth is necessary now. She quietly sings the opening and goes first. We climb through after her.

Much has changed. As Kerin told us, there's a break, a rift, in the bubble that contained the wasteland. Dead air, dry and flat, blows through the tear in the barrier. The air is less thick than normal; there's less water in it. Ocean water that bled through before has mixed with dry dust from the wasteland, coating the ground with a strange mud. There are patches that look like burn marks.

A shriek sounds in the distance. I freeze; we all do. It isn't human, it isn't even siren, it's something altogether different, and the noise sends a spike of ice through my middle.

"The scouts—quickly." Lyrionna crosses the short distance to the to the rift, starting the song. The other Aerers join. There is a breathless quality to the song, and I realize that hot dry air must affect those born in Araem.

Ellie gestures to Mom and me to listen as she adds her voice. I pick out the song's melody, and hear its complexity. As it takes shape in sound, I see it form in the air. Ellie nods to us, and Mom and I join in. Our singing is not as strong, but when we add our voices, the visual song thrums with the extra help. Plus, we don't seem to be affected by the drier air. The sound filaments reach out to the rift, lashing onto it and pulling it together.

Beyond the barrier, about halfway inside of the wasteland, is the other tear with its shredded edges. This tear leads to the world of The Underneath. As I watch, it bulges, filled with a gel-like substance. It's like an elastic liquid-filled toy ball I had when I was younger. You'd squeeze it and one side would pop out, as if it were about to burst. The gel bubble expands in the ripped window until I am sure it will explode. But then an edge falls out and the rest wriggles through. It's one of those creatures. A scout. It's as large as the shadow I saw in the water with Macon. Its thick flesh looks transparent and with its diamond shape, it reminds me a little of a manta ray. But its body is thicker, less graceful. It lashes its blunt tail and starts toward the rift, rippling across the dusty ground almost as if it's flying.

The song catches in my throat. Ellie shakes her head at me, gesturing to keep singing. I point to the scout inside the wasteland. The others have noticed it now, too. Lyrionna increases the intensity of the song, the threads move faster.

A second scout is through, this one even bigger. They shriek. My mouth dries, but I still force myself to sing. They ripple toward us over the scorched ground. They're fast. Another scout falls through the gap; this one tearing the window wider. And then comes another. They shriek again, the sound rattling the rift.

We almost have it. The barrier breach is nearly closed again. My body strains with the effort of singing, with the struggle not to run screaming. Then behind us is an answering shriek. It is much closer than before.

I glance behind me and another scout is rippling toward us. Where the undulations of its body touch the ground, it looks as if the color has been sucked out of the vegetation. It isn't just color, it's the life-force of the vegetation, of the very ground, being leached away. Pulses of energy shoot up from where it touches the ground and are sucked into its body, making it more opaque. But only briefly, as if it's burning through the energy as fast as it takes it in.

It's killing everything it touches, consuming it, burning its way toward us. Kerin has noticed as well, and without pausing in the song, he draws his weapons and stands ready. Araline joins him, lifting a long knife made of stone.

The scouts inside the wasteland press against the rift, pulling at the stitches of song holding it together. More of them pour through the tear inside, rippling across the ground and piling on top of each other at the barrier, layer after layer of thick transparent gel. There are so many that they rise up above us and spread across to either side. The rift bows out toward us, while the scouts shriek and crush against it. More and more are coming.

The song changes abruptly, and I spin around to see that Araline is on the ground, hurt. The scout she was fighting rises up above her in an arc. She thrusts her stone knife upwards, puncturing its body. It shrieks again, a different tone, and trembles. This causes a frenzy in the creatures on the other side. They renew their efforts, pushing against each other and the barrier. The scout Araline stabbed falls forward. Kerin leaps to pull her out of the way, but it's too late. The scout lands on her, its body covering hers completely. Kerin stops singing, frantically trying to shift the creature's weight and narrowly misses getting hit with its swinging tail.

I can still see Araline through the body of the scout. Her mouth and eyes wide, her stone knife pinning them both together. The red of her skin and bronze of her hair fades as the ground around them turns to ash grey. The scout is fighting death, pulling everything it can from Araline's body and the surrounding area. Kerin plunges a staff into it, and it finally stops moving.

I think I might throw up. The others see what's happened but don't stop the song. Lyrionna continues to sing, strain showing on her face now too. Kerin's voice cracks as he picks the song up again. Behind us there's another shriek, and then another, and another. Still more scouts are coming from behind us. Obviously more than two came through the rift after Kerin and the others left. The ones pressing against the barrier are piled so thick, I can hardly see past them. But inside the wasteland, something else steps through the tear. It looks like a tall, impossibly thin human made of opaque glass. Its face is indistinct, but its mouth stretches wide as it screams—not in fear—more of a cry of triumph. Carrying a spear-like weapon, it moves so smoothly that it glides across the dry wasteland earth. Two more just like it follow closely after.

The first humanoid skims toward the rift, the scouts falling back to let it pass. It reaches the barrier and tries to push a hand through the edge of the closing hole. Lyrionna directs the song to lash over its hand, pulling the edges of the rift together. The humanoid jerks back and changes tactics, thrusting its spear against the still-repairing hole. As it hits, a *boom* cracks through the air and the ground shakes. It thrusts the spear again and the hole that had nearly closed, rips with the sound of tearing cloth.

I look from the barrier to the other scouts advancing from the rear. I count at least five there. We're about to be caught between them and those at the rift. We have to get out of here. Kerin stands ready with his weapons held high, facing the creatures advancing from behind.

It isn't going to work.

If we stay here, we'll be trapped. The creatures behind will pick us off one by one while the humanoids and other scouts rip through. We aren't stopping anything. We have failed. I grab Mom, and she returns my terrified look.

Ellie must realize it too. She pulls Lyrionna, Odele helping her.

"Kerin, come on!" I shout at him, but he firms his stance in response.

The opaque humanoid hits the rift again, shaking the ground and tearing more. Lyrionna snarls.

"Mother! It's too late. We cannot win. We have to try another way."

Lyrionna shakes free of Ellie but shouts for us to go. Kerin won't leave Lyrionna's side, angling his body to try to cover the dual points of danger. Mom stumbles, and Ellie picks her up. I put Mom's arm over my shoulder to help take her weight. We've backed up to where the window to the ocean was.

Then a new earthquake hits and the rift splits again, spilling gel creatures into Araem. I see Lyrionna and Kerin beyond the writhing mass of creatures sliding through the barrier. Ellie sings to open the window into the ocean and pushes me and Mom through. Then she sings to close it behind us.

Her eyes are the last thing I see.

Chapter 38

I scream for Ellie, but nothing is there, just ocean. Fear and worry for Mom pulls at me. I have to get her to safety—whatever that is. A blast shakes us in the water, and Mom is ripped away from me. I grab for her shirt before the blast current can send us in opposite directions. Her T-shirt rips. I can't see her anywhere. I call for her, using my underwater voice.

Another blast shakes the water. I look back and see with horror that there is something unraveling in the ocean fabric; the window into Araem is tearing again. I see flashes of gold and silver and a cloud of red before it closes again. No, no, no — "Ellie!" I shout. The next blast launches at me. The water is hot and light, shot through with steam.

I hesitate only for a second before Mom jerks my arm. She found me again. "Swim, Cam!"

We go. I don't want to leave the water, but I focus on getting Mom to land. Once she's safe, I'll come back.

Song bursts through the water, a different tone and melody but similar to what Lyrionna does. I think she must be using it to fight. It's followed by a shriek from one of the scout creatures. Underwater, the cry sounds as if it's laced with fire as it hits my ears. We press on and break the surface off the coast of Shell Island. We've been gone long enough that darkness is beginning to fall—if it's even the same day.

I signal to Mom and go back underwater. We're much faster swimmers under here—at least I am—than on the surface. I pull Mom with me. We don't come up again until my feet brush sandy ground and waves push us toward the rocks.

Macon and Bridgette stand on the rocks at the surf line, calling to us. Their gestures and voices seem as frantic as I feel. I give a last push of effort to reach them. Macon snatches at my hand and misses as a wave retreats, dragging me backward. When the ocean pushes us forward again, he grabs at me and braces himself to pull me up. It must be hard because I'm still holding on to Mom, and the waves are pulling us back. Bridgette helps too, and we finally splash onto the rocks. She's still wearing my clothes so either it's the same day, or they haven't left. I help Mom to stand before turning to scan the waves for any sign of Ellie, of any of the others.

The sea moves strangely; something is building underneath.

"Get up! Go, now!" I shout.

We scramble as fast as possible to get to the top of the bluff. I scrape my hands on the rocks and bang my knee. There's enough salt water streaming down my face and clothes that the stings last only a second before healing. Small mercies.

At the top, I look back again. Fear pools in my belly as my mouth goes dry.

"What is that?" asks Bridgette, her voice barely above a whisper.

The ocean is drawing back—as if it's building for a

massive wave—but it's pulling unevenly, strangely. It's parting—pulling on each side—revealing the shredded edges of a tear in the ocean wall. Scout creatures flop through the break, ripping at it as they did in the wasteland.

No! This can't be happening.

Where they touch the ocean floor, steam rises and the sea floor turns grey. Their bodies pulse with energy. It's what they did in the siren world, sucking the essence from the earth.

I think I see the glimmer of Kerin's copper hair, as song rises above the noise of the water and the eerie cries of the scouts. The song pushes against the creatures as if it has substance, like it's a weapon. The water crashes back, hiding the tear. The sea is in turmoil.

It parts again and one of the opaque humanoids swipes with its spear.

"Oh my God, Momma!" screams Mom.

There in the melee is a flash of gold and silver, of pale iridescent skin. The sea falls inward covering the break again. I can't see Ellie, Lyrionna, or anyone. Macon laces his fingers tight with mine, his solid presence next to me helping a little.

"Cam, sing," orders Mom, eyes still fixed on the thrashing sea. "Listen to me."

Mom starts a song, her voice unsteady. It's a calling song, I somehow know. I trace the melody with my ears and add my voice when I think I have it. I see the song stretch across the water, diving underwater, looking for its target. She is trying to call the others to us.

But it's not right. Or it's not enough.

A line forms under the water, steam rising, grey splotches forming around it. They have broken through. They are on the move, and they are heading straight toward us.

.

Chapter 39

"Something is coming!" shouts Bridgette, terror cracking her voice.

Dread roots me to the spot. I lose the song, my throat too dry to sing. Mom and I can't fight this alone. There's no sign of the others. Mom sobs. My mind rushes to Ellie—her cryptic comments, fierce nature, and otherworldliness—my grandmother. I thought nothing could ever sway her, that nothing could dare hurt her. And Lyrionna—a force of nature, although there was nothing natural about her. She has the power of all the siren disciplines; Ellie had said: "everything and more." Even brave Kerin is lost under the waves. I cannot believe that they all may be gone; my mind rejects the very idea.

But The Underneath comes.

The creatures, scouts and humanoids, seem to be moving across the ocean floor. The water is disturbed above and around them. At the sight of it, fear and adrenaline rip through my body. There's nowhere to run—nowhere to go. The water isn't safe, and we live on an island. Even if we could make it to the mainland, that doesn't mean they won't follow us, won't spread out across the entire world until there is nothing left but dead, dry air and dust.

We stand linked—Mom, me, Macon, and Bridgette— holding on to each other as if together we're stronger. And we are. Mom and I can't sing the Aerers' barrier song as well as they can, but we know it. If only the other two could help us, but Bridgette is human. Macon though… I look at him. His eyes are fixed on the sea at the inevitable force advancing. There's still enough sea water in my eyes to see his inner glow, and pieces start to fall in place.

Macon is something else.

"The clearing— Macon, we have to go now. We have to go to your tree."

He looks at me with wild eyes.

"Cam? What are you talking about?" asks Mom.

But there's no time to explain. We need help. There is a reason The Underneath is coming here of all places. The stories had things in common. If I'm right, we may still be able to fight.

Bridgette screams. The first of The Underneath creatures are close enough that we can see them rising out of the ocean. Cold panic washes over me, and I know everyone must feel the same.

A humanoid crouches on the back of a scout, its spear held high. Its impossibly wide mouth opens, filled with teeth like broken glass. It lets out a crashing roar, as if urging the others on. Steam rises around it. Behind it, more creatures rise, the line behind them growing and thickening. The first is almost to the rocks. And then it will climb.

"Trust me— Come on, please!"

They don't need any more encouragement to run.

"The clearing! Go to the clearing!"

I hope I'm right.

WE CRASH through the brush and trees, all of us together. We burst through the trees into the clearing and realize we're not alone.

"Macon! What are you doing?" Anne shouts. "Bridgette? Thank God. Where have you been?"

She and Rob are standing there, looking at us goggle-eyed and mouths agape. We don't have time to explain everything —no time to get yelled at.

Anne rushes at Macon, taking him in her arms. He pushes free.

"Mom, you and Dad have to get out of here. Get Jack and take a boat. Go to…" He looks at me helplessly.

I can't answer. There's nowhere to go. There's only one thing I can think of and it's not even a full thought. "Macon—your tree."

"My what?"

"The tree. You didn't come here when you were a few months old. You were *born* here. On this island and I think—maybe right here."

Anne claps a hand over her mouth. Macon turns his questioning eyes to her.

"There's no time, Macon," I say. "You heard the tree, you heard her. She knows you. We need help."

"I—I…" he starts, and then something shifts in his face. He snaps his head toward the tree, as if he hears something. Then he turns back to me as if he's made a discovery. "I have to wake her up." He looks as if he can't believe what he's saying.

North of us is a crash. The Underneath creatures have

reached the forest. Bridgette huddles with Anne and Rob trying to tell them what's going on.

"Hurry!" I say, hauling Macon with me to the tree. *His* tree. The tree that sometimes flashes with his glow.

He nods, places his hand on the bark, and closes his eyes. Then he opens them and looks at me with naked fear. "I can't. Nothing is there."

"Yes, you can. Listen. Tell her to help us."

The shock of touching this tree knocked him out the first time. Then when he woke up, he heard her. That was the first time. What am I missing? What changed? Then she went quiet. But he heard her warning in the clearing earlier.

He cries out and doubles over as if in pain. There is another crash to the north. We can see trees sway in the distance. The creatures are bulldozing toward us, trees falling in their path.

I wrap my arms around Macon for support.

"It hurts. The trees are hurting," he says through gritted teeth.

"Stop this!" Anne cries, but Mom keeps her from rushing us.

He's hearing his tree—or hearing the forest—but we need her to *wake up*.

And that's it, of course.

I start to sing. It's born from Ellie's complex melody. The song she used to heal Miron and Kerin, the song she uses to treat the hides, the song that I sang to Mom in the hospital, and the song I sang right here the day the tree spoke to Macon for the first time. Siren commands don't work on Macon, but maybe the song actually did. Maybe it can work here. I place one hand over his, the other on the bark, and sing for all I am worth. I feel the living essence of the tree, its connection with Macon. I sense his entreaty to her to wake. We're connected, the two of us, and he with her.

"Hello?" says Macon.

The tree sighs. It shivers. And a face appears under the bark, rising to the surface. It's exactly what I hoped, but I still cannot believe what I am seeing. Eyes, nose, mouth and brow rise through the bark. Shoulders pull free and I drop my hand from the trunk, as the tree-person reaches for Macon. I feel the reverberations of that touch shoot through him into me.

Macon takes her hand like an old-fashioned gentleman and helps her step away from the casing of the tree. She stretches, as if waking from a dream. Her skin is the color of split pine, her hair is bark brown and her eyes are deep green, ringed with brown. She's covered by a dress that looks to be made of woven pine needles mixed with bark—only it's soft —and whispers against her skin as she moves. Macon watches her, breathless. She is lovely. She looks into his face and smiles.

"We need help," I burst in, interrupting the moment.

As I say it, another crash reaches us as a tree breaks in The Underneath's path. The tree-woman grimaces as if it causes her pain.

"I know." Her voice is creaky but clear, and her green eyes seem determined.

"What did you do before? How did you defeat The Underneath? They are coming now."

Macon looks at me with surprise, and I hear Mom's intake of breath. All the stories had elements in common, and I am certain that the woman before me was a key part in them. Macon's face is full of wonder but not disbelief. I think he hears the truth in what I'm saying, even if he may not fully understand.

More crashes from the north, and the tree-woman flinches

again. Mom is at the ready. Bridgette and Rob seem floored, Anne frightened.

"Sing, little girl," says the tree-woman, laying a rough hand at my back, pushing me forward. Her touch is a jolt of energy that I feel from feet to crown.

"Mom!" I call and she is there beside me, starting the song.

"Get behind us," I shout to the others.

I add my voice to Mom's trying to replicate the song of the Aerers. We move forward to the north end of the clearing with the tree-woman at our side. I see our song build in the air at the tree line, weaving a net. We're not as strong as the Aerers. It will be like trying to stop a hurricane with a tissue. But we have to try. As though we had rehearsed it, we sing the net into a curve, widening as it moves away from the top of the clearing. We need to block and also corral the creatures coming for us.

We press forward, the song interlacing through the trees ahead of us, using them as sort of anchors. I look for the tree-woman. She is kneeling on the ground, hands spread in the grass. Then my focus is straight ahead as the first of The Underneath creatures comes into view. It's an undulating scout with a humanoid crouching on its back. Behind it are more scouts with humanoids riding them. The ground under them is mottled with grey. They have razed a path through the forest to get to us. The first humanoid raises its spear and gives a shout when he catches sight of us, poking the end of the spear into the scout's flesh to spur it on faster.

It runs smack into our song net, invisible to its eyes. It shouts in fury and strikes out with its spear toward us. The spear hits the resistance of the net, and I'm jolted as if it had hit me directly. The humanoid screams, wide mouth gaping.

More humanoids are piling up, joining the first, banging spears against the net. Please let it hold.

Then tree-woman lays her hands on our backs and something moves through me again, stronger this time. It's better than coffee or adrenaline; it's the pure energy of life, of growing things. It bolsters Mom and me, and our song builds in complexity. The tree-woman walks between us to the front. She takes my hand, moves it to Mom's, and then covers them both with hers.

Then she kneels back down to press her other hand on the ground. I feel our connection strengthen, filling with force as if she is calling on the forest—the whole island—to help. But there's just so many of The Underneath. They strain against the song net, pulling at trees. The ground where they've stopped turns greyer, releasing fine, dead dust into the air.

Macon takes my free hand. At first, I think he's trying to let me know that he's there, give me someone to lean on, but I feel another rush of support. It's not as strong as the tree-woman, but it's tangible and fierce. Then Bridgette's there, then Rob, and even Anne. They lay their hands on us, too, adding their strength. It's only a whisper compared to the tree-woman and even Macon, but the show of solidarity brings tears to my eyes, and it helps.

Mom and I sing and sing. It seems that we have them contained, and despite their constant attacks at the net, it's holding. Without pausing in the song, I catch eyes with Mom. I can see the strain in her body and face and am sure I must look the same. I ignore it—can't think of that right now—because the next step has to happen. Now that we've stopped them advancing, we have to get The Underneath off the island.

Mom nods her head once, showing me she understands my unspoken thought. We squeeze the hand of the tree-woman, and she rises. There's a brief lull in the added power, but then it comes back. She seems to have switched channeling from her hand to her forward-planted foot. I grip Macon's hand and jerk my chin forward to point north. He seems to get it and nods.

Then we all advance one step. Macon's parents and Bridgette stay with us. Then another step. We move together and as we do, we push the net away from us. Not only do Mom and I have to sing to keep the net strong and together, we will also need to cinch it in toward itself to catch The Underneath creatures in its trap. It's a balance of pushing them away and trapping them inside the song net. We'll funnel them toward the ocean and then back through to Araem and the tear into their own world.

The humanoids scream in protest, beating their spears against the unseen net. The scout creatures bang against what they cannot see. Like flies against a window, bashing their buzzing bodies against the glass, not understanding why they can't move through. Although The Underneath creatures seem to know exactly who, if not what, is stopping them. Their gazes go straight to the tree-woman.

We advance once more, Mom and I singing to pull the net together to channel them back toward the sea. I'm not sure how we can continue to push with this strength when we reach the sea. I wonder if the tree-woman's force can help us where no trees grow. And the humans can't follow us underwater. My brain races, as we push forward again. The scouts pile on each other against the sides of the net, creating more pressure for us. They shriek and flail. A humanoid falls off its scout and is lost in the fray until it cuts through scout bodies to get to the top again. The dying scouts begin to fade and curl like paper near a fire. Others pile on top of them as if to consume their energy before they disappear. The dying ones become more opaque as they disintegrate, sloughing off into fat grey flakes adding to the dust. The others lose interest as soon as there is nothing more to take from their bodies.

We move forward another step. We've reached the edge of the forest. My feet scuff in grey dust, powder fine. It coats my still-wet sneakers. But where the tree-woman steps, the grey fades and is replaced with spots of green, like new grass. Her verdant footsteps lead us into the what used to be thick forest.

Her strength is not as powerful as when we were in the clearing. If she's still pulling from the forest using her feet as the contact point, then walking through the dust must dampen her power. Or she just has to reach deeper. But the spots of grass still appear under her feet, so something is working.

We advance, tightening the net, shoving it forward. It's slow going and exhausting. Each blow from the spears shakes us. The weight of the creatures strains the net. And still we press on, step by step, until finally a gust of ocean air blows into my face. I fill my lungs with salty air tinged with pine. It's like splashing my face on a hot, dry day. A cool glass of water after a restless night, an apple at eleven o'clock when you forgot breakfast. That extra push, when you are sure you have no more to give. We can see the ocean, but we're only halfway to our goal.

Then Mom stumbles. I feel it through her hand and as a stutter in the song. At that second, a humanoid thrusts its spear against the net and it jars me, rippling out into our group. Threads of our song snap. I see it happen. I try to sing harder to make up for it, but the humanoid spears the net again and we are all shaken. It has made a hole in the net. My mouth dries and the song falters again.

The tree-woman snaps her head toward me and sends a ribbon of energy to me and Mom. I feel it, but it's weaker than before. A spear hits again and more threads snap. The point of the spear breaks through the song. The humanoid in front thrusts a hand through the hole and reaches for the tree-woman. Macon shouts and drops my hand. The song stutters again. I fling my arm in front of the tree-woman, beating Macon to doing the same. The humanoid clamps down on my wrist.

Chapter 40

The song dies in my mouth. From somewhere, I think I can still hear it, but it's faded and very far from me. Time seems to slow as everything drops away. I'm encased in a cloud, numb.

My eyes are fastened on where the creature's hand circles my wrist. Slow pulses of energy go up the creature's arm— energy from me, from my body. Each pulse takes a little more. I can feel myself weakening. I think of Araline's open eyes, of her fading away while the dying scout absorbed her. This creature is very much alive, though. It's becoming more solid-looking as my energy feeds it.

Pulse. Pulse.

Something tugs on my other arm. I vaguely register that it's Mom, trying to pull me away. Arms go around my waist and someone tries to lift me. Macon. But I am rooted to the spot. From somewhere there is muffled shouting. My knees buckle, but the creature doesn't let go. Arms tighten around my middle. I barely feel it. Everything is so very far away.

Pulse. Pulse.

I'm hypnotized by the sight of my life force leaving me.

The edges of my wrist are turning blue. It reminds me of Lyrionna's mark, except the blue is a different color.

Pulse. Pulse.

I could fall into that blue, as if into the sky. My vision narrows. I'm folding into myself, the world retreating. Sounds fade. My body is heavy, encased in molasses. I'm slipping. All I can see is blue. This blue looks like dying.

Pulse. Pulse.

I blink. No. I can't die here. This isn't right. I can't— I *won't* let go.

I cough and then take a deep breath. Salt and pine, ocean and forest—family and love. It sizzles through my lungs, and I search for the threads of song. I hear Mom's voice.

I blink again and fully come back into my body.

My wrist is in agony. Macon still holds me, but the tree-woman and others are crowded around Mom. She is carrying the song on her own, bolstered by the others' energy. No one is directing energy to me. Of course not. Because the creature would just absorb it.

The net still holds, despite the hole. Mom's kept that from getting any bigger. The Underneath creatures press against the humanoid holding my wrist. I glance at Mom, and her face is a mask of pain. Tears stream from her eyes as she keeps singing. The salt tracks down her face leave pearly trails, and her eyes swim with siren colors.

The sight of her face sears into my mind as I look back at the creature gripping me. My wrist throbs, but the pulse of energy slows. In part because I don't have much more to give, but also because I won't give any more.

This is not how I go down.

The creature's hand covers Lyrionna's mark. Another example of someone else's will taking mine away. My anger kindles, spreading through my body. It catches like wildfire running through my veins. My very human anger floods through my body.

Pulse.

No more.

"Stop." It's a siren command, coming from deep within my bones and more powerful than I have ever given. I twist my wrist—or try to.

The creature screams but does not let go.

Commands don't work on them.

I reach for the Aerer song but then have an idea. I want to recreate Lyrionna's song that she used to lift Ellie's mark. I don't know the exact melody, but I'll use what I remember and if I can direct it right at the mark... As the song builds, a new pain lances my wrist. It curls underneath the creature's hand, and the humanoid screams again, finally letting me go. A spiral is burned into its palm.

I sag into Macon's arms and then quickly add my voice to Mom's to close the hole in our net. Now that I'm free of the creature's grasp, the tree-woman reaches for me again, and I feel the rush of her power. Macon also lends his strength to mine, to ours. We're weaker than we were before, but it's enough. It has to be. We push forward again.

Then I hear the most beautiful sound in the world, another voice, rising up to join our song, and then another—harmonizing and weaving. They add to the song, strengthening the net and pushing The Underneath farther back and into the ocean. We move forward several steps. Another voice joins and then another, then more. Some sing our song, others are slightly different, but it somehow buoys ours. We reach the rocks, still singing, still pushing.

In the sea, spreading out on either side of the net, faces appear. Metallic hair, shining skin and voices—beautiful, glorious voices—rising up to join the song.

We start to descend, the tree-woman leading our group. I squeeze Macon's hand trying to indicate that he should stay on the ridge.

He shakes his head. "Nope."

He won't stay, and his parents won't let him out of their sight. Bridgette shakes her head too. I look at Mom, helpless. What are we supposed to do with a load of humans underwater?

Then the ocean parts, peeling back like the Red Sea in a movie, making a narrow corridor around the netted Underneath creatures leading toward the tear into Araem. But it isn't Moses standing there. Lyrionna, eyes blazing, hair swirling around her head, has arrived. Leaning heavily on her is Ellie. Their voices join our song.

Chapter 41

Now we are able to press all of The Underneath creatures up to the breach leading into Araem. Sirens step out of the waves, joining our bizarre singing procession. Lyrionna drops out of our song and sings her own, opening the passageway wider, singing it into a massive window big enough to herd the creatures into Araem. We follow behind them.

The net pushes them all the way to the rift in the barrier at the wasteland. As we get close, they surge back towards us, and we have to brace for the pressure. The humanoids fight hardest against the net, led by the one who had taken so much from me. Even as weak as I am, the spear hits have less impact now. I still feel them, but they don't rattle my bones anymore. The extra voices diffuse the effect. Bridgette speaks to Rob and Anne, explaining the world, I think. They both seem beyond awe.

Now we're here, we're faced with two tricky steps: we have to get them through the barrier into the wasteland and then force them back through the tear into their own world.

The hole in the barrier is huge compared to what it was before, but The Underneath creatures didn't come through as one army. They came through one or maybe a few at a time. We'll have to sing-shape the net to force them back through the rift while making sure we don't compromise the barrier itself. We can't have any more of the wasteland air and dust blowing into the siren world. The air in this area is even drier now than it was last time.

The only good thing with that is it isn't affecting Macon as bad. He isn't gasping… not yet. I'm a little worried about the sirens, though. Their skin is losing some of its sheen; they're drying out. I hope they can hold the song.

Pulling together, our song weaving and growing, we push the net against the barrier and into the wasteland. The edges of our song fill the rift and stop the dead air coming through. About half the contained creatures are inside the wasteland, the rest are on the other side of the barrier. They rail against the net.

We're not done. We can't let them loose inside the wasteland, they'd just rip through again. We have to get them out of Araem altogether. But how? The tear leading to The Underneath is even smaller than the rift in the barrier. Lyrionna could sing the tear wider, but it's so deep into the wasteland I'm not sure her song could reach it. And I don't know if she would be able to hold the song if she went directly into the wasteland herself.

As I'm trying to puzzle it out, the tree-woman turns to me and Mom. "I must let you go now. I can help in another way with this transition."

When she removes her hand, I feel her force go with it, but with the other sirens singing, we can still maintain the net. It's harder, but it holds. The tree-woman approaches Lyrionna, gesturing to the wasteland. Lyrionna shakes her head at first, but the tree-woman scoops up some wasteland dust that had blown through and holds it out to her. Then the tree-woman places her other hand to the ground. The handful of dry, grey dust softens to the same reddish-brown color of the ground.

This seems to convince Lyrionna. She helps Ellie to sit, then shouts to us. "Hold them. Hold the net closed!"

We tighten the end of the net together, corralling The Underneath creatures within it, holding it steady. Lyrionna concentrates on a separate section of the barrier, singing a hole just large enough for the tree-woman to slip through into the wasteland. Then Lyrionna pulls the hole tight but not completely closed. It forms a snug circle around one arm of the tree-woman. She kneels in the grey dust; little clouds billow up around her in the dry air. The hand on our side touches a patch of ground untouched by The Underneath. She buries her other hand in the wasteland dust and concentrates.

The area around her knees begins to change. The dust settles and the ground starts to take on a reddish hue. She's doing the opposite of The Underneath creatures—transferring life back into the ground instead of leeching it out. Just as she helped us in the clearing, she's using the power of the earth to move energy where it's needed.

Then she moves a few feet backward closer to the tear leading to The Underneath's world. As she works, Lyrionna sings the arm hole to follow her progress, so that the tree-woman can keep one arm on our side. I see it now. She's creating a "clean" path for Lyrionna to follow to get to the tear.

My attention lurches as a hit reverberates through me. One of the humanoids presses against the net nearest the tree-woman. Screaming, shouting to her in what I guess is their language, beating its spear against the net over and over. Some of the other humanoids pile toward her as well, but many still strain toward us—focusing just to my right. I catch eyes with Macon. He seems to have noticed too.

"What are they doing?" He shouts to me.

I can't answer without dropping the song, but I jerk my head toward the tree-woman.

He follows my gaze. I point to him with our clasped hands and to the tree-woman. He frowns. "Me? What can I do?"

I don't know for certain, but I'm sure he could help somehow. We lock eyes and something unspoken passes between us. He looks thoughtful for a moment and then seems to come to a decision. As he lets me go, our collective energy dips a little bit. We adjust and hold the song steady as we can. Macon rushes to kneel by the tree-woman's hand pressed to the ground outside of the wasteland. He hesitates a second, as if he has no idea what to do, then reaches down to lay his hand over hers. She jumps at the contact and looks up. When she sees it's Macon, she smiles with clear adoration. It makes a difference, too. Her work goes faster, the reddish-brown earth spreading out around her like spilled ink.

Every humanoid now shifts its attention to where Macon and the tree-woman are. They climb over each other, desperate to reach them. Their screams almost drown out the song. The scout creatures flop about trying to get close as well. We sing, straining to keep them contained. Someone's voice cracks but quickly rises up again. Just a bit longer.

Lyrionna keeps pace with Macon and the tree-woman's progress, her song adjusting the barrier until they finally arrive next to the tear leading to The Underneath's world. They've created a corridor of good ground straight through the wasteland, changing the dome shape to accommodate it. Lyrionna gestures to the tree-woman and sings the arm hole large enough for her to step out of the wasteland. Then Lyrionna pulls the hole tight so that only a tiny opening is left, just big enough for her to sing through.

She turns back to us and nods her head. Somehow, we all seem to know what to do. She will widen the opening to The Underneath, while we push them inside with our net. We'll have to line the net up with the tear, open the end, and use the net to force them back into their world. We'll have to do it without allowing anything else to escape from The Underneath and without letting more of the wasteland air blow into Araem. I firm my stance. We are ready.

Lyrionna's song changes as she sweeps her hand as if she's opening a curtain, and the tear expands into a large window. We sing over her, bending the net with our voices, moving the edge of it over the opening. Something moves within, but I try to ignore it. Sweat drips down my cheek. Lyrionna's song changes again, and I see that she's attaching the wasteland barrier to the edges of the new window. Now the only thing separating us from the world of The Underneath is our net. My heart kicks up a notch. We slide the edge of the net into place over the window, flush against the edges.

Once in place, I risk a glance at Mom. She's staring at Ellie, sitting on the ground with her eyes closed. I have a moment of panic, a wobble in the song, but then force my eyes away. We have to stay strong now.

Mom tightens her grip on my hand. We focus back on the net, peeling the song back from the end, creating a funnel into The Underneath's world. Some of the scouts fly back through immediately. Some still press against the net, directly in line with the tree-woman, desperate to get to her. She and Macon stand together. In the strange light of Araem, they both glow as if lit from within.

The tree-woman reaches out to Lyrionna, laying a hand on her arm. Lyrionna flinches, but then grasps back, and she joins our song. We have another rush of power shoot through our connected song. We squeeze the net from our end, pressing and pushing. The humanoids fight the hardest, but they are no match for all of us, working together. Even Macon's parents and Bridgette are still supporting Mom and me. I can pick out each of their particular energies, giving us extra strength.

We contract the net more as we force them back through into their world. Lyrionna drops out of our song as the last few are shoved inside so she can work on closing the window. I feel the loss of her voice and the tree-woman's power as she does. Lyrionna is working incredibly fast weaving the window closed. It takes longer than normal, and I realize that she is taking extra measures with this seal. She is fortifying it as well as sealing, as if adding steel bars to an already-locked bedroom window. I'm fascinated with her skill. The window and net close together. We drop the net as the last of The Underneath creatures is forced through, still babbling in their odd-sounding language and screaming in frustration or anger, maybe both.

Lyrionna's weave is finished except a small opening the size of a dessert plate. She sings the weave, and as it's closing, one of the humanoids grabs the edges and tries to pull in opposite directions, face against the opening, glass-like teeth gnashing. There is a tearing noise and a cry from behind me.

We dropped the net too soon.

My throat aches from my singing, but I add my voice to Lyrionna's song anyway. She flicks her eyes in my direction as if surprised, but her concentration is on repairing the hole. I think I'm helping, but the creature keeps pulling at the edges. As it tries to reach through the hole, I see the spiral burn in its palm.

I don't think about what I'm doing. I'm not even sure I

know what I'm doing. I drop out of Lyrionna's song and create a new one. I sing it sharp and direct, aiming at the grasping fingers and open mouth. It flies home, precise as an arrow, hitting the creature and knocking it back. Lyrionna finishes her weave, and the hole closes completely as if there was never a passageway there. Then she closes the tiny hole in the barrier. It shimmers, intact again. The barrier that's no longer a perfect half-circle dome, after the tree-woman's efforts in reclaiming a sliver of the land.

A cheer rises all around. Ragged sirens surge around our group. They thank Mom and me, touching our hands. They surround Rob, Anne, and Bridgette in frank fascination, running hands down their arms and over their hair. Bridgette laughs good-naturedly but Anne and Rob flinch away, probably still adjusting to walking through to a new world. I catch Anne look with despair at Macon and the tree-woman standing together, hands clasped. He gazes at the tree-woman in wonder.

I hug Mom tight, and we hurry through the crowd until we reach Ellie's side. Lyrionna is already back with her, brushing her hair off of her face. Mom falls to her knees calling to Ellie.

The world drops away from me; I'm transfixed with fear for two breaths. Then I am down on my knees next to her as well.

"Ellie? Ellie? Grandmother, wake up!" I'm afraid of her shallow breaths.

She opens her eyes and looks to Lyrionna and Mom and then me, and ghosts a half-smile.

"We have to sing for her," I say, and start us off.

Lyrionna is right behind me, and then Mom too. Together we sing, quiet and intense, Ellie's melody. I feel a warm hand on my shoulder. Macon has come to join us. His added strength swims through me. Our song reaches out to her, sinking into her body.

Ellie moves, breathes deeply, and fully smiles now. "I think that is enough, I am not such a wilting flower."

WE GATHER AT THE CAVE, which I find out now isn't a prison, it's where Lyrionna receives guests. Not that she ever made me feel like a guest, per se. Lyrionna "gives breath" to Macon, even before he starts to struggle as the air becomes denser with the barrier closed and the tree-woman's healing. She gives breath to the tree-woman as well, who says her name is Alice.

"Alice? Really?" I can't help exclaiming. It's what the birth certificate said, but it's such a normal name for such an extraordinary person.

"It is the name given to me most recently. My actual name is..." and she makes a rustling, sighing noise like the wind in pine needles.

"Okay then, Alice, it is."

She can't stop smiling at Macon, and touching his face. He notices his parents and calls them over. Rob still has a blank look of shock. Anne's expression is more complex. It seems she's fighting with herself, some inner turmoil under the surface.

Macon introduces them to each other, as if they've never met. Alice touches their cheeks and says, "I could not have chosen better. You have done so well."

Anne tears up, and Rob puts an arm round her shoulders

"She's my birth mother," Macon tells me.

"I figured. Um, what is she?"

"I don't know— A tree spirit?"

"What does that make you?"

"I guess the same old boring guy as ever."

I laugh. If there's one thing Macon has never once been, it's boring.

Bridgette is talking to Kerin and Odele and the other guard we had, Kiyash, Kerin's brother. They look like they've been in a war, but they're standing. A weight lifts that I didn't even know I was holding. I don't know them well, but I am profoundly grateful that they are okay. Mom sits next to Ellie, holding her hand and fussing. It must be a change. I realize then that Mom isn't using her cane.

Someone gives us a clear liquid to drink—water with a hint of an unknown fruit. I drink three glasses straight in a row. It soothes my parched throat and refreshes me, while Lyrionna and Ellie fill us in on what had happened when The Underneath first broke through—both into Araem and Earth. They stayed to fight, and Ellie was injured. Lyrionna took her back into Araem, creating a window in a different place. Odele followed them. Then they realized that there were still people left in their community, but they had been cut off from the wasteland area by The Underneath creatures roaming around there. The creatures hadn't strayed far from the area near the wasteland. Odele went to search for others, looking for the rest of the Aerers—or anyone—to help with the fight. Lyrionna wouldn't leave Ellie but made it back to the area outside the wasteland to see if there was anything she could do to try to stop The Underneath invasion. That's when she heard us and came to help.

She adds, "By then there were no creatures from The Underneath left by the wasteland. They did not try to take over this world. Their only focus was to break through to yours."

"To find me," says Alice.

She has our attention. I'd had an inkling about this, but I want to hear her story.

"My kind are connected to life, to trees and grass, vegetables and fruits, and all that grows and dies to nourish new growth—the cycle of life. That place, the creatures there, they grow very little. They have learned to take—from each other, from the essence of their world. They consume life—take everything they can. It cannot be sustained."

She pauses for a sip of her drink and then continues. "I was captured, so long ago now. They used me to bolster their world, themselves. They wanted my life force, my essence, to use it. I can replenish with life, but they sucked it away faster than I could tap into it. I was there a long time."

The memory seems painful. It sounds horrible to be used that way—like food.

"When was this?" asks Macon.

"I do not understand time in same way as you. To me, it was a very long time ago."

Long ago for her is hard for me to wrap my head around. No one here was alive then. The sirens only know the stories passed down through—what, generations? Wow.

"I managed to escape to this world. Your people were kind to me," Alice says to Lyrionna. "I was very frail, and while I was recovering, those creatures broke through looking for me. Many lives were lost. Only by working together were we able to beat them back and close the passageway. As we did today." She looks around at everyone gathered, everyone who played a part in this victory. "Your kind built the wall around the destruction they caused. But I could not help repair the land, for I was too weak."

She pauses and takes another drink. "I am so very sorry that it happened again."

The sirens around us whisper in low voices. They must

realize that they are in the presence of a living legend. The stories that they grew up on had truth to them. It'd be like sitting down and having a chat with Paul Bunyan or Sleeping Beauty and getting what really happened in their lives.

"I have had a long rest in my home, in my tree, and I am recovered. Now I can help you heal the land beyond the barrier."

There's even more excited whispering around the room. They seem to love the thought of reclaiming the wasteland.

"We would be honored," says Lyrionna. "How can we help?"

"When you have rested and healed, you could sing the waking song." She turns to me. "Just as you did, so I could hear my son through my deep slumber. So he could ask me to leave my tree."

I feel everyone's eyes shift to me and then to Macon as they understand who she means by son. Anne blanches. Mom's eyes widen.

"We can do that," says Lyrionna, eyes narrowed and calculating as she looks at me.

Then she addresses the room. "Those who know the healing songs, help your sisters and brothers. Go to your homes, rest and sleep in peace knowing that we have defeated The Underneath today. When you are revived, I ask all Vivoem to help. And anyone who knows the song and can lend their strength. I expect some of the others will come as well. They cannot have missed what has happened here."

What others? I wonder.

People move around embracing each other, helping each other, as they prepare to do as Lyrionna asks. Many stop by us to thank us again, and look in awe at Alice. The large room empties out. Odele and Kerin are the last to go. Odele approaches me with halting steps.

She speaks in a low, urgent voice to me. "Forgive me, Camline, I only did as I was bid, but I did not want to break your trust. Please take these and forgive me."

In her outthrust palm are the pearl earrings that Blue gave me, the ones I had bargained away for Odele's help last summer. I try not to snatch them, but I am so glad to see them. *Mine.* I rub my thumb over the pearl and it sends a delicious zing through my middle.

"Thank you." I smile at her. I don't blame her anymore. How can I? Lyrionna is a force to be reckoned with.

I look over to Bridgette. She's wearing both her earrings as well.

Odele turns, but I catch her arm. "Who was Lyrionna talking about? What others are coming?"

Odele looks puzzled. "The rest. Our other sisters… and brothers." Then her eyes widen. "You did not think we were all there was in Araem?" She gives me another unbelieving look and laughs as she walks away.

I guess it makes sense; that'd be like Kerin thinking that all of Earth is Shell Island.

Mom is frowning in curiosity at Macon. She shifts her eyes to Alice, to Macon's parents, and back. I can see her trying to work out what I've been wondering myself but was too shy to ask Alice. Mom seems to have no compunctions.

"Macon is your birth son?" Mom asks her.

"Yes." She seems very pleased with this.

"Who's his father?"

"Mom!" That was a bit blunt. I cringe at Macon, but he just looks interested to know the answer.

"He was beautiful. His name was James and he helped me recover when I escaped. We spent a season together, but my tree called me and I could no longer wait."

Macon and I share a glance. That makes no sense. Macon

is seventeen years old. Alice escaped hundreds of years ago. Mom seems confused as well.

"But— He's only just a kid."

"Time has different meaning for my kind. I carried him in the long, slow time of a tree. I woke when he needed to be born, but then I had to finish healing in my tree. He is very like his father, so he could not stay in the tree with me. So, I found you." She smiles serenely at Anne.

"Mom?" Macon asks.

Anne reddens. "It's true. We found you in the clearing with Alice. You were so tiny." She smiles a sad smile. "I promised to look after you, but in the beginning, you needed so much more than I could provide by myself. Miss Ellie helped us, helped you grow strong enough so that I could take you home." Then she adds in a reluctant voice, "She also helped us when Child and Family Services came to check on you and review your birth certificate. After talking to Miss Ellie, they completed it and signed everything off. We adopted you. We told everyone you were born elsewhere."

So Anne and Rob have known about Ellie's power—been afraid of it—for a long time now. When did they find out? No wonder Anne didn't want Macon seeing me. She was scared of me, of what I might be able to do. She didn't—doesn't—know he's immune. Whatever Anne knew about what Ellie can do, it doesn't seem as if she shared it with Bridgette's mom. Bridgette had her own crazy theories about us. She had either misunderstood or heard different stories from her grandmother who had been in love with and rejected by my grandfather, Oscar.

Macon's face is troubled as he looks from his Mom to his Dad. "Why did you lie to me? Why not tell me the truth?"

"I was afraid of this! Of losing you. Now you'll go back with her—you'll disappear."

Macon's eyebrows shoot up, and Alice laughs, like pine needles rustling.

"What are you talking about?" he says. "You're my Mom, Dad's my dad, Jack's my brother. We're a family. I can't just leave. My life is in the world—uh, our world."

Alice caresses his cheek. "Nor could you live in a tree, my love. You are too much like your father. You do have something of me in your eyes. And maybe in here." She lays a palm over his heart. "I hope you will continue to visit me."

"Of course," he tells her, faint color stains his cheeks. Then back to Anne and Rob, "You should have been honest with me. I would have handled it."

"He's known about me since last summer." I offer in a small voice. "You took that pretty well—better than I expected."

"You knew?" Anne asks. "And how do you know that she didn't... doesn't... make you..."

"Mom, please don't finish that sentence. Give Cam some credit. Plus, it doesn't work on me."

"Ah! That is from me." Alice seems very pleased. "You cannot command me, unless I wish to agree."

Lyrionna listens with interest to this. She regards Alice and Macon with what seems to be guarded respect. Then her eyes pass over the humans, Ellie, Mom, and land on me.

Ellie speaks up. "You should rest too, Camline. Take these others and your mother and go home."

It's not a bad idea. I'm shattered, even after the refreshing drink they gave us. Mom has deep hollows carved under her eyes. I hope she hasn't pushed herself too hard. Not that we had a choice.

"What about you, Ellie? Are you staying here?" I ask.

Ellie glances at her mother. "I will stay to help heal the land, to be with my sisters again, but I will return."

I say goodbye to Alice, and she embraces me. Her limbs are hard as branches. She smells of pine sap, lush grass, and coastal air.

"Stay strong, little singer."

Her face is unreal, beautiful, and as alien as Lyrionna's who walks up to me.

"Thank you for what you did, Camline." Lyrionna's voice catches on my name. "You—you wear that name well." Then she changes the subject. "You can see the song of the Aerers."

"Yeah, I guess so. Can't everyone?"

"No, only those with the Aerer gift. And you know the song of waking. You can use it."

"Ellie's song? I can't sing it as good as her, but I guess I can sing it well enough sometimes."

"You sang something different to stop that creature from tearing the hole as I closed it. Something that had a physical effect."

"I was just trying to help." I shift under her stare. She's looking at me with the same scary interest that she had for Macon the first time we were here together. "What?"

"I would like to know more." She says it lightly, and steps away.

I go to Ellie and wrap my arms around her. This is not a normal interaction for us, but after today… "What was that all about?" I whisper to her.

"You show gifts for many songs, and for songs we do not know. That is not usual. I told you that you were strong. I just did not know how strong."

I did use a version of Lyrionna's song on the humanoid creature. I glance at my wrist and the mark that Lyrionna gave me is still there; it just looks darker. I ignore it; there's something else I'm curious about. "What was that about my name?"

"It means 'song.'"

"That's all?"

"It was also my grandmother's name." Ellie traces a finger across my eyebrow and cups my cheek. "I will see you soon."

A family name. Mom never said. I glance at Lyrionna and wonder what her relationship was like with her mother.

Lyrionna meets my eyes. "Come again soon, Camline."

Well, that feels ominous.

Chapter 42

Lyrionna walks us to the window into the ocean and creates a tube of dry air in the water to let us walk back to the island.

I check in with Bridgette on our way back. She's managing pretty well, though she seems a bit dazed about the news of Macon's heritage. Rob and Anne won't let go of each other. Rob stares at the watery roof above us. It is pretty impressive. It must take less effort than to "Red Sea" it again. Anne keeps trying to hold on to Macon, but he slips from her grasp a couple of times before he finally stops.

"It's okay, Mom. I wish you'd told me. It would have explained a lot, but… we'll be okay."

"I know but you ran away last week, and I was so scared."

Oh, right. They don't know that part of the story. "We didn't run away," I say. "We were *there*. Uh, for maybe an hour and a half." He and I exchange a look. "I probably should warn you, time moves differently when you're in Araem. That's what it's called. We may be missing some time when we get back."

Anne looks as if she can't take any more revelations right

now. Macon smiles at her. "It's gonna be okay," he says again.

The sea closes behind us as we move. Shortly, we reach the coast, climb up the rocks in the half-light, and start toward the clearing. I check the position of the sun. It's evening, not morning, but I don't know which day.

You'd think I'd be used to the weird and wonderful by now, but I can't stop marveling at Alice's green footsteps in the river of grey dust as we pass them on our way. The dust lies as a reminder of the horror from earlier, but her living footsteps look like hope.

My phone buzzes as it links up to unseen satellites. No water damage. I'm back in service. I check my phone for the time and, more importantly, date.

"Hey guys, it's Monday evening. We've missed school again. Bridgette, your parents are going to be freaking out."

"I'll speak to your mother, Bridgette," says Anne. "Unless you want to tell her… something?"

She blows out a breath. "*Non*. Maybe not yet."

"We'll just say that we lost service, and that we needed you."

We all laugh. It's the truth.

Bridgette gathers the forgotten bag with her clothes, and Mom picks up her cane from where she dropped it last. We exchange raised eyebrows and tentative smiles over it.

Anne offers for Bridgette to spend the night at their house. She can sleep in Jane's old room. Anne will speak to her mom and they can wash her clothes in time for tomorrow. Macon says he'll bring her over to my dock in the morning so she can get her boat for school.

School. Really? It feels a million miles away.

I hug Macon chastely—our parents are right here—but I whisper in his ear. "Are you okay? With everything?"

"You mean since I learned that my birth mom is, you know, a tree? And that my birth dad has probably been dead for—I don't know—centuries? And that my parents lied about it all this time? Yeah, I'm dandy." He rubs his face and grimaces a smile. "I'll be okay, honest. Just gotta think about it a bit more."

"Okay grandpa pine."

"Touché, siren girl."

"Right."

"See you."

⁓

As Mom and I make our way down the path by the light of my phone, I see that I have a lot of missed texts from Blue and Dad. Blue says she's sorry she freaked, it was a lot, and she definitely wants to talk, she's calmed down now, but am I ever coming back to school?

Dad is more succinct: ***Where are you?***

I have three of these, timestamped for today, plus some emails over the last few days that I skim. He's sure I've heard he's going to seek custody, we can talk about it but it's for the best, stop ignoring him, where the hell am I? He went by my school, he's going to speak to us in person….

"Oh no," I say, as we're leaving the forest.

"What, honey?"

"I think Dad might be…"

Before I finish, we see him. He waits on the doorstep of Windemere, looking like he's spoiling for a fight.

"I'll talk to him, don't you worry, Mom." A spark of anger ignites, as tired as I am.

"No, Cam, we're—"

She doesn't get to finish, because Dad sees us and gets to

his feet. He looks me over, then Mom. "I don't know what the hell is going on here, but you two are ignoring me, and Cam missed school again. They said that they didn't even get a phone call before they 'remembered' that they weren't supposed to give me any information? This stops now."

I am about to shout back, but Mom's voice cuts through, cold and clear.

"Thomas. That's enough. Now let's all go inside and we'll discuss."

I open my mouth to protest, but Mom shakes her head. "Now."

She opens the door and we both go in after her. She sets her cane down just inside the door.

"Sit down, both of you. I am going to make some tea and heat some stew."

"I'll help you."

"No, Cam, I've got this. You two just wait a moment."

Dad looks confused. He stands by the door like he doesn't know what to do with himself. I sit down at the table. My eyes follow Mom as she gets down mugs and bowls, then takes a pot out of the refrigerator and sets it on the stove. She fills the teakettle and sets that on the stove as well. She leans against the counter and crosses her arms.

"Go on, Thomas, sit down."

He blusters, but when she doesn't budge, he finally sits.

"Now, Cam and I have had an extraordinarily stressful and exhausting…" She looks up and to the side as if calculating the time, or just trying to figure out how to finish the sentence. "…day. We need food and we need rest."

Dad starts to speak, but Mom holds up a hand.

"I understand that you have questions and that you have been worried. We will answer as much as you want to know, but I want to be very clear about something from the start: Cam isn't leaving the island unless she wants to. Period."

"The courts may feel differently about that," Dad says evenly.

"They might. Until I speak to them. Or Cam does."

He frowns at us. "What kind of threat is that?"

The kettle whistles and Mom takes it off the stove.

"Chamomile okay with everyone?" she asks, pouring the water without waiting for an answer. "Thomas, do you still take honey?"

"What? I don't care." She watches him impassively. "Fine, yes. Now, do you want to explain what you meant by that comment?"

Mom delivers the tea to us, and then goes back to the stove to check the stew. She ladles some into bowls before she answers him. "I think the bigger question is, do you really want to know?"

"What is that supposed to mean?"

She walks over with two bowls, setting them down in front of us.

"Exactly what I said. It's your choice, you get to make it. You live in a regimented world. You like to know what's going on and you like to control situations. There was much you didn't want to look too closely at when we were married." He opens his mouth as if to protest. "You know it's true. I'm not finished speaking." He presses his lips together.

She returns with her bowl and spoons for all of us.

As she sits, she says, "As I said, I'll tell you anything you want to know. I'll tell you why Cam has been missing school. I'll tell you why I didn't call today. I'll tell you why never again will someone make Cam do something she doesn't want to. But you can't hide from the truth. You can't pretend you don't know where I come from and what I am. What Cam is."

Dad huffs a laugh, looking between us both. "What kind of nonsense are you going to spin this time? And you've gotten Cam mixed up in it too?"

Mom says nothing, just stirs her stew and lifts a spoonful to her mouth. She blows on it and then takes a sip as she watches Dad. I'm transfixed. I've never seen Mom talk to Dad like this. She's so calm and so poised.

"Cam, eat your stew, you'll feel better."

She's right. As soon as I take the first swallow, I feel a bit more restored, a little less frayed. Dad hasn't touched his.

Mom goes on. "Thomas, I could tell you that Cam is a delinquent and has no regard for authority and that I can't handle her. I could tell you that we can't survive without your support, financial or otherwise. I could tell you that I need you and can't live without you. I think you'd believe me if I said those things, but they would be lies. Now, it's your choice. Do you want to leave here tonight believing those lies or do you want the truth?"

Dad's face reflects his military man stoicism. His back is ramrod straight and a muscle jumps in his cheek. He's wary, like he's going to be caught in trap. He turns to me. "Cam, are you just going to sit there slurping your soup?"

I should be furious by now. After his emails, the letter he sent Mom, the showing up out of nowhere after years of basically nothing. But seeing Mom so composed seems to have had an effect on me.

"Dad, this may be difficult to understand, but right now, I need to eat this stew. It's a restorative for us." I take another bite as if to punctuate my words. The stew is helping. I'm still tired, still can't wait to sleep for hours, but I don't feel like

I've been peeled off the pavement anymore. Like someone who sang a net to trap a whole army and nearly died for it.

I go on. "And I think Mom's asked a valid question. You can go on believing what you think is happening, continue with your court 'whatever,' and I'll resent you, but it won't make a difference in the long run. I'm staying here right now. This is where I need to be."

Dad's mouth is set in a thin line. He's still angry, but at least he's not shouting. Why is he here now after all this time, anyway? But as frustrated I may be with him, I can't hate him.

"Dad, I want you in my life. I've missed you. I was really mad that you left us when Mom and I needed you the most. That hurt." A lump forms in my throat and I feel my eyes prick with tears. I risk a glance. His head is bowed. I lower my eyes. "Do you want to know what's really going on?"

"Yes."

I place my hand on his arm, eyes razor-sharp in the salt of my own tears. There is no denying what I am with my eyes like this. I see true and can be seen. His sandy-brown hair is clipped short and has more grey in it now; there are more lines on his face. It's all heightened in my eyes. Despite everything, he's still my father.

"Dad, look at me."

Chapter 43

"Cam! You're going to be late if you don't hurry," Mom shouts through the door the next morning.

"Be right there!"

I finish brushing my teeth while I think about Dad.

We told him everything—well, pretty much everything. I didn't go into specifics about all the dangerous bits—decided I should leave some things for later. I also didn't tell him about Macon's whole deal. That's his story, not mine.

Dad didn't believe me at first, thought my siren eyes were a trick of the light or something. I really didn't want to risk laying a siren command on him to prove it. Miss Wren's languid attitude and druggy look was still fresh in my mind. So, I sang him a little of the Aerers' song, and he tapped on empty air to find it solid.

We talked and answered his questions until Mom said I really needed to sleep because I was definitely going to school in the morning. Mom said goodnight to Dad, and I walked him down to the dock.

He said that Mom was looking good, and then—complete shocker—told me he was sorry that he wasn't there for us, and he'd try to make up for it. He said he'd be stateside for a while, and we should keep talking. I told him I'd like that, and it was true.

We'll see how that turns out.

I wipe my mouth and stare at my reflection. I don't even look like myself. My skin and hair shine, but my face is too thin and I have dark circles under my eyes. The good bits must be a side effect of being in the siren world. The bad bits are from fighting for our lives.

I finger comb my hair into some semblance of neat, gather my bag, check for my phone twice, start to leave, and then run back because I forgot something important on my bedside table. I slide it into my pocket and kiss Mom before I run out the door.

Macon and Bridgette are already pulling up to the dock. I run down to meet them. We all give each other appraising looks and nervous laughs. Everything is so unreal.

Bridgette's boat has a bit of water on the floor. Probably because of all the sea partings and inter-world fights happening a half mile or so away. But it starts fine, and Macon helps her get it untied before we leave.

"So," he says, as he pilots the boat toward Williams Point.

I slide in next to him, wrapping my arm around his waist. He feels so solid and real to me, so right. "Yeah?"

"We had a weird night. We told Jack everything. I hope that's okay? We had to explain where everyone was and why we weren't answering any phones."

"How'd that go?"

"Well, he's started calling me 'Sap.'"

"Sap?"

He makes a face. "For 'sapling.'"

I laugh—musical, and high.

"Watch it, your siren is showing."

"C'mon, Sap is kind of funny. But he accepted it all?"

"After a good hour and a half of him demanding that we stop pulling his leg. I think we wore him down. I showed him my birth certificate."

"I was thinking about that—your mom's last name."

"My mom—I mean my Mom-mom—ugh, I mean Anne and my dad gave that to her."

"I wondered about that."

"You caught it too? 'Alice L. Carroll.'"

"Like Lewis Carroll, right? Alice in Wonderland, *Through the Looking-Glass*?"

"Yeah. They're hilarious. I guess my, uh, birth dad called her Alice, but they never got around to a last name. They had to have one for the birth certificate."

"I like it. No info about your Dad, though."

"Just the name 'James' and that's only because she told me. Guess they really weren't big on last names. How was your night?"

"Funny enough, about the same. And speaking of fathers… My dad showed up and now there's no pretending we're normal anymore."

I tell him about the conversation and how badass Mom was. I explain about the court letter that Mom received and how Dad must have had some inkling in the past because he never let us go to the water—not that he admitted to that.

"And of course, the whole crying thing."

Now it's hard to remember that I spent most of my life being unable to cry because Mom so was afraid of people knowing what I was that she sang a block on me. Then I remember something else. "You know, Macon, I think maybe we did kind of start the breach this time."

"Really? I was a little afraid of that, but I don't understand it."

"You saw how The Underneath was so fixated on you and your—Alice?"

He nods.

"They started to attack in earnest when you and I were there, but then they calmed down after we left. Then they started up again—on Saturday."

"You think what happened when…?"

"Yes, I think that was when the tree—Alice—started to wake up. When she started to speak to you, they could sense it—her—more. The attacks started again and were worse."

"Okay, but why did they break through when you and Bridgette were there?"

"I have a theory or two." I reach into my pocket. "One, the window was already weakened and the 'tides,' as they call it, had pulled the worlds closer together, and two, I had this with me."

I open my hand to show him the carved seahorse. "Maybe they could sense you, and therefore her, through this. I mean, you put a lot of yourself into your carvings, maybe some of your essence gets into it. Plus, I'm willing to bet that you got the wood from the clearing. Maybe even from Alice's tree?"

He looks thoughtful.

"It's just a theory."

"So, you carry that with you wherever you go?" He grins.

I roll my eyes but smile. "That's your takeaway from what I just said?"

Soon we arrive at Williams Point. Bridgette has already tied her boat up and gotten out.

Macon maneuvers his boat up to the dock. I help him get it secured and jump out. He hands me my bag and joins me. Bridgette waits by the road, head bent over her phone.

When we turn, Blue is standing there. I'd texted her last night to say that we'd chat later and that I was coming to school. I didn't really want to tell her anything more over text. I guess I should have expected her to come meet us, but it takes me a minute to recognize her because her hair is chestnut brown. Plus, she's wearing a plain, dark jacket instead of the acid green one I'd teased her about before. She's carrying three coffees.

"Hi," I say. "Is that for me?"

"Yeah and one for you, Macon. Um, can we have a minute?" She hands the coffee to Macon with a sheepish look for making him leave, I think.

"Thanks for the coffee." I take a sip and stifle a grimace. Pumpkin Spice. Well, it's the thought that counts.

As we both look at each other for a silent second, I am struck by even greater remorse. I have to try to make this right. "Blue, I'm so sorry. I shouldn't have said anything. And I didn't know that Lyrionna, that lady, was going to show up like that."

"No, oh my God, *I'm* sorry. I told you a thousand times that you could talk to me about anything. I thought you were having trouble with Macon. Or that it was going, you know, *really well* with him and you were thinking about notching up a level. Or that your Mom was sick again. I—I had no idea."

"I get it, I'm sorry. It's a lot to lay on a person. I just wanted you to know. But if it's too much, I could… help… with that."

"No!" She says it so forcefully, I'm taken aback.

Then she continues in a softer tone. "I don't need that. It isn't too much, not really. I just needed some time. It was freaky, okay?" She lowers her voice even more. "And Bridgette kept making comments about you and then Miss Wren was acting loopy…"

"That was a mistake. I didn't mean…"

"I know. That's what I'm trying to say. I know you well

enough that you wouldn't hurt anyone—not on purpose. But I had to work through it to get to that place. And I needed to do that on my own. I'm sorry I didn't answer your texts over the weekend."

"You're sure you're okay?"

"Yeah. I am. But I. Have. So. Many. Questions." She spaces her words as her eyes light up, and she breaks out a mischievous grin.

"Wait, I have one question."

"Okay?"

"The hair? Your clothes? What's going on?"

She flushes. "It's my right to express myself by any means I want. And I needed a little less extraordinary for a bit after Friday."

"Fair point. It does look good on you, Bluebell." We walk up toward Macon and Bridgette.

"Breaking out the full name already… I see how you are."

"Uh huh. We should go."

Macon takes my hand and interlaces his fingers with mine.

"All good?" he whispers.

"All good," I whisper back. Then louder, "Come on, Bridge, get off the phone, we're going to be late."

She looks up and grins, sliding her phone into her pocket.

Blue looks startled. "Wait— We like her now?"

I smile. "Uh, yeah. We have a lot of catching up to do."

EPILOGUE

We head back to the island after an interminable day at school. I told Blue a bit about what happened in snatches between classes and when the others weren't paying attention at lunch. She's taking it… okay. I'm not sure how much she thinks I'm making up. Macon's quiet agreement helps. He hasn't said a word about his birth mother, though. I get it.

After our last class, I made the executive decision to stop by DJ's to grab lobster roles to go. I'm ready to eat mine right the heck now, but I'm being good and waiting. I'm so tired, I can't stop yawning. The normalcy of classes and homework was unreal after the last few days. Macon says I should rest. He doesn't seem any less tired than me though, so I hang out with him as he drives.

I put my hand on his shoulder and focus on the horizon. The boat skims over the sea, bumping over waves. I've talked myself out and am happy just to sit in silence, lulled by the droning of the engine.

The sky and ocean seem to merge together in the distance. In the afternoon light, I can hardly see where one ends and the other starts, the blues and greys overlapping and mixing together like a painting. Low clouds add to the illusion. It looks as if it could go on forever, like a hallway of mirrors. The horizon line is indistinct and muted, marred only by a smudge of soft black. My eyes are drawn to that, puzzling out what it could be. It's out of place, interrupting the flow of water and sky. We're heading right toward it.

"Macon…" I squeeze his shoulder and stand up. There's something inside that dark patch.

"What is that?" He's seen it now, too.

"Slow down." I can't take my eyes off the smudge. An iridescent shimmer swims over the surface as we get closer. Macon slows the boat and steers us out of the direct path. There is definitely something inside—a boat.

"Is that…?" Macon's voice fades as he stares at the dark patch.

"Yeah." I see it now for what it is, a window. The darkness is the sky of wherever the window goes—it's night there.

The picture flickers. I lean toward it. The person at the helm looks up—and through—to us. I catch his surprised eyes. We must appear in a shock of light to him. As he opens his mouth to say something, the window disappears in a blink.

Macon eases completely off the throttle and we float next to where the window was. Nothing is there now, just waves. I drop heavily into my seat. I can barely breathe, and my hands shake.

"Cam?"

"Oh my God. Macon, it was Oscar. That was my grandfather."

THANKS FOR READING

I hope you enjoyed *Landbound* as much as I've enjoyed sharing it with you.

If so, would you be willing to leave a rating or review (on Amazon, Goodreads, BookBub, etc.)? Reviews are the best way to help other readers discover new authors. I am sincerely grateful for every one I receive.

WANT TO KEEP IN TOUCH?

Join my Readers' Group to be the first to know about fun news and info, new releases, and giveaways. Just pop to my website www.daniellebutlerwriter.com and sign up. I'd love to see you there!

ACKNOWLEDGMENTS

First of all, thank you to my readers! I'm so grateful to you for giving a new author a chance with *Watermarked* and for continuing on with the series. I appreciate you all so much!

Although writing can sometimes feel like a lonely task, getting a book out takes a mini village.

Thank you to Keith Bailey who helped with boat terminology and sailing advice — any mistakes are my own. Huge thanks goes out to my first readers, Paige Beeman, Mandy Fischer, Christina Garner, and Elizabeth Luce, your insights and thoughts made all the difference. Also extra mention to Christina for advice and support in this crazy business.

Thank you to my amazing editor, Amanda Saint, for helping refine and finesse the telling of this story. Thank you to Three Point Author Services LLC for proofreading and rooting out errant Anglicisms.

The cover was designed by Jennie Rawlings of Serifim who found a way to visually, and beautifully, express the heart of the story. I love it so.

Massive thank you to my extended, blended, and growing

family. We're all a little crazy; we all know it, and I love us for it.

Finally, my most heartfelt thanks goes to Matthew Lange, who always has my back and still will stop everything to let me read something out loud to clarify my thinking. And he made the 2020 lockdown a bit more bearable.

ABOUT THE AUTHOR

Danielle Butler has spent most of her life making up stories. From the rich and multi-layered lives of her Barbies and anthropomorphised stuffed animals, through her work as a long form improvisation and stage actor to development producing for film and TV—it was all about What Happens Next. American-made, she lives the exPat life in the UK with her husband and various pets in a little house on a very old river.

daniellebutlerwriter.com

facebook.com/DanielleButlerWriter

twitter.com/DSButlerWriter

amazon.com/author/daniellebutler

goodreads.com/danielle_butler

ALSO BY DANIELLE BUTLER

Watermarked

Printed in Great Britain
by Amazon